MARY PRINCESS OF AYRI

By

Linda Tilley

This book is a work of fiction. Places, events, and situations in this story are purely fictional. Any resemblance to actual persons, living or dead, is coincidental.

ISBN: 1-4107-7090-7 (e-book)
ISBN: 1-4107-7091-5 (Paperback)

This book is printed on acid free paper.

1stBooks - rev. 07/18/03

Acknowledgements

First I would like to thank my friend and editor, Barbara Jackman for working so hard on this project and Catherine Kirby-Grove for reading the first pages and encouraging me to continue. Phyllis Meade gave me valuable insight and feed back after reading the first draft to her students.

And finally I would like to thank my mother, Ruby Parcell and my husband Joe for their unfailing support and encouragement.

Chapter 1

Mary Smith didn't really like her name. It was so plain and ordinary.

But, she thought, *I am plain and ordinary so I guess it fits me.*

She didn't know that she was anything but plain and ordinary. In fact she was extraordinary, as she would soon find out.

Mary rested her chin on her crossed arms and turned her head to stare out the school room window. It was late afternoon. She was bored with the math lesson and had already completed all her homework, but she dreaded the dismissal bell's ring because then she would have to go home.

Mary's home was not the warm loving place that she had read about in her library books. Her parents were cold and aloof and Mary was convinced that they didn't love her at all.

All too soon the bell did ring and Mary sighed as she slowly gathered her books and made her way through the classroom door and down the hall to the exit. A group of her classmates had gathered just outside the exit, talking and laughing. Mary dreaded walking past the group and wished she were invisible. They were whispering and giggling as they watched her approach. She braced herself for the taunts that she knew they would shout as she walked past.

"Carrot top, carrot top, here comes carrot top. I'd rather be dead than red on the head!"

Mary pretended to ignore them but their foolish words hurt and she felt like crying. *Why does everybody hate me?*

Mary was smaller than most of the children in the fourth grade with large blue eyes and a multitude of freckles sprinkled across her nose but the first thing anyone noticed was her brilliantly red hair. Mary knew why the other kids made fun of her and it wasn't the color of her hair or the thrift store clothes her mother bought.

I just don't fit in, she thought. *I don't have anything in common with them. I don't watch TV and I'm not good at sports.*

Another problem was she was far more intelligent than all the other children. The school officials had even wanted to place Mary in a special program for gifted children at the State College but Mary's parents would not allow it.

Mary remembered the scene at home when she gave her parents the letter from the teacher about the special program.

Mary's Mother barely glanced at the paper and handed it back to Mary. "Tell your teacher you will not participate."

"But why," Mary pleaded, "I really want to go!"

"I have made my decision. You will continue with your education at the local school."

"The teacher said it would be a good opportunity for me. I don't understand why you will not let me go."

"Mary, there will be no further discussion. Now go to your room."

So Mary stayed at the elementary school and endured the taunts of her classmates.

Mary's teachers tried to keep her interested but they couldn't devote as much time as they would like. This special treatment only made the other children dislike Mary even more.

Mary silently endured their jeers and ridicule as she walked to her bus. She valiantly struggled to hold back the tears that threatened to fall. *I will not let them see me cry*, she thought as she climbed aboard and sat down.

On the long ride home Mary tried to read but she was too sad to concentrate. Seeing the happy children being greeted at their stops with hugs and kisses by their mothers and fathers hurt more than all their taunts and unkind words. She could not remember ever being hugged by either her mother or father. When the bus finally came to her stop there was no one waiting for her.

As Mary trudged down the long dirt road to her home she wondered again why her parents didn't love her.

Perhaps they don't love me because I am so different from them…so ugly, she thought as she pictured her parents.

Mary's parents, George and Carrie Smith, were the picture perfect couple, tall with lovely dark hair and beautiful brown eyes. They were always neatly groomed with every hair in place.

Both of them have perfect skin without a single freckle, Mary thought. *They must have adopted me, and now regret it.*

As Mary walked slowly along the gravel road she became lost in her favorite daydream of a warm loving family, doing all the things that she had only read about in books.

Get real, girl, Mary thought. *It would be nice to have a real family instead of the parents I have, but I don't. They don't care anything about me. I wish they would just go away! Maybe then I could find a family that would love me. I'm not so bad even if I am ugly.*

Lost in her thoughts, Mary almost walked by the friendly little rabbit that hopped out to meet her almost every day.

"Oh hi little one. I'm sorry I almost stepped on you," she said as she bent down and reached out her hand.

Mary knew that it was not normal for a wild animal to trust a human, but for as long as she could remember the animals in the forest around her home had been drawn to her. *Just another sign I am a freak,* she thought as the rabbit moved closer. It gazed lovingly up at Mary and she lifted him up and gently cuddled him in her arms. She looked down at the small animal and sighed contentedly as she rubbed his tiny head and brushed back his silky ears.

"You are such a sweet little rabbit," she cooed. "You love having your ears rubbed don't you?"

Mary closed her eyes and held the little rabbit close.

"Did you know that you and the other animals in the forest are only living things in the world that love me?"

The tiny rabbit snuggled closer as if he understood her words.

Glancing at her watch she said, "Oh my, I have spent far too much time here. I have to go now. You better get back into the woods far away from the road because it's too dangerous for you here. Besides if mother ever saw me petting you we both would be in trouble. I don't know why she doesn't want me to have any pets. I guess she doesn't want me to have any friends at all, especially wild animals."

With one last rub behind the ears Mary sat the rabbit down beside the road and pushed him toward the bushes. She knew she would have to run to get home on time. Her mother expected her home at exactly the same time every day. Mary didn't want to explain why she was late. When the house came into view around the last turn in the road Mary slowed down and walked the rest of the way.

"Good afternoon Mary," her mother said as Mary entered the kitchen.

"Good afternoon Mother," Mary answered and put her books on the table next to a glass of water. It was the same routine every day after school. She was expected to drink the water and then go to her room and do her homework. Mary didn't bother to tell her mother she had already completed her homework because Mother always had the day precisely scheduled and didn't tolerate changes well.

Mary finished the water and went to her room. For exactly one hour she pretended to do her homework.

At the end of the hour Mary took her homework to the kitchen and gave it to her mother.

"I'm finished with my homework, Mother."

"Very well," Mary's Mother said and began to read Mary's work. After a few seconds she said, "I do not find any mistakes, Mary. You may take this to your room and place it with your books. When you return to the kitchen please start your exercises."

Without a word Mary picked up her papers and walked to her room. *I'm so tired of this same old routine,* she thought as she placed her homework on the desk in her room. *You would at least think she would say I did a good job or something. She never changes her tone, even if I make a big mistake. I guess I should be glad she isn't mean, but sometimes I think it would be better if she were. Anything but just cold and distant. She just doesn't care about me at all!*

Mary went to the living room and climbed on the treadmill and set the timer for 20 minutes. She was so lost in her thoughts that she didn't hear the bell that signaled the time was up until she heard her Mother speak.

"Your exercise period is at an end, Mary. I have checked the print out on the treadmill and you haven't been working up to your full potential. You must work harder."

"Yes mother."

"You may go the kitchen now and I will serve your food."

Mary's mother placed the food on the table and left the room. Mary always ate alone in silence. Her parents never sat down to a meal with her.

Once, after hearing at school that most families ate together, Mary asked, "Why don't you and Father eat with me?"

Her mother answered "There is too much work to be done before your early bedtime. We will consume nourishment later when the work is done."

Mary sat down and started to eat. The food was bland and boring. "Corn, carrots, mystery meat, one slice of bread and an apple. What a surprise, it's the same old thing I have every night," Mary said with a sigh. She didn't know her mother had returned to the kitchen until she heard her speak.

"I have prepared your food to be nutritious and it contains sufficient calories for a growing girl. It is neither old, nor the same every night. For example, last night you had potatoes and peas with your protein and fruit. If you are having difficulty with your memory, perhaps I should include memory enhancing exercises in your schedule."

Mary, turned to face her mother and with what she hoped was a convincing smile, said, "No thank you, mother. I remember perfectly well. I am sorry if I have troubled you."

"I am not troubled," she said and turned to leave the kitchen.

No, you never are troubled. You never get excited or mad, Mary thought.

After eating Mary cleared the table, washed the dishes and put them up. She cleaned the kitchen and when she was finished her mother kept her busy with other chores until bedtime. There was always something for Mary to do and most nights she would go to bed exhausted.

Even on the weekends Mary's mother made sure she was kept busy. On a typical Saturday she would be awakened early and given a long list of chores to be done. In the afternoon she would follow her mother on a long hike into the forest that surrounded their home. Mary had to pay close attention to her surroundings and the direction they traveled. When they had gone deep into the forest her mother would tell Mary to lead the way home. Her mother explained that this training would keep Mary from getting lost if she ever ventured into the forest alone. Mary thought this was ridiculous. She was never allowed outside alone. Just how her mother thought she would wander off and become lost was a mystery to Mary. It was a sad and lonely life for Mary but she was strong and managed remarkably well to endure her dismal life.

The only time Mary was truly happy was at night when she would dream of a wonderful sunny place where she was free to run and play. Sometimes she would dream of a beautiful red haired woman who would hold Mary in her arms. The woman would sing a beautiful melody but Mary couldn't understand the words. She felt so loved and warm in her dream that she would be sad to awaken and find herself in her hard, cold bed.

As Mary prepared for bed she thought about her wonderful dreams. *I hope I have good dreams tonight. I feel so tired and anxious. I wonder why.*

Chapter 2

Mary lay awake for a long time and when she finally drifted off to sleep she was abruptly awakened by a loud noise. She sat up wondering what had happened when an explosion rocked the house. She jumped out of bed and ran to the window to see what was going on. There was an orange glow coming from the orchard and what looked like a lot of people running toward the house. There were brilliant flashes of light and thunderous explosions shaking the ground.

Mary's bedroom door flew open with a bang and her mother said, "Mary, come with me. It is imperative that you leave here immediately."

Mary was so shocked by the loud noises and her Mother's sudden appearance in her bedroom that at first she couldn't move.

"What's going on?" She managed to say as her mother took her by the arm and pulled her to the door.

"You are in danger. We must move quickly."

Mary pulled away and cried, "I have to get my clothes. I can't go out in my gown."

"Leave them, we have to go now. You are in danger."

They ran down the steps, out of the house and into the forest, with Mary's mother practically dragging her.

"Where are we going?" Mary managed to ask her mother.

"You must be quiet."

Mary tried to keep up but her bare feet were being cut and bruised. She felt as if her lungs were on fire and her legs ached. She managed to carry on for a while but finally she could go no further.

"Mother, please stop!"

Without a word Mary's mother picked her up and ran on deeper and deeper in to the forest. Mary could not understand what was happening. How could her mother move so fast through the forest in the dark? Mary was still out of breath but her mother was moving faster and wasn't even breathing hard. Mary was terribly frightened.

"Why are we running though the woods? What's wrong?" She cried.

"You must be quiet. We need to get to the escape vessel before they find us," Mary's mother whispered.

"Who's after us and what escape vessel?"

"Remain quiet Mary. There is no time for explanations."

After what seemed like hours they came to a solid rock cliff reaching high above them. Mary's mother put her down and turned to face the cliff.

Mary asked, "What will we do now? We can't get over that."

Her mother didn't answer but began searching the face of the rock and when she found a small outcropping she pushed with a force that Mary didn't know her mother possessed. Much to Mary's surprise a door made of solid rock opened in the cliff's face and her mother ushered her inside a large cave.

There was a faint greenish glow coming from deep in the cave. Her mother pushed her ahead toward the light. The sides of the cave were rough and rocky but when they at last came to the source of the light the walls were as smooth as glass. The room was perfectly round and in the center sat a huge metallic cylinder. The greenish light was spilling out of a door in the side of the cylinder. Mary tilted her head back trying to see the top of the cylinder but it reached far up into the blackness above. Mary's mother pushed a knob on the wall and the opening through which they had just come slid closed.

Mary stood shivering in the cold damp space and said, "I'm cold Mother."

Her mother ignored her plea and said, "Mary, follow me quickly. We do not have much time left. Father will only be able to delay them for a short time."

They went inside the cylinder and then her mother closed and sealed the door behind them.

They were in an area that was filled with pipes, wires and metal boxes with small lights that blinked. In the center there was a ladder that disappeared upward into the dark.

Mary's mother pointed to the ladder and said, "You should be sufficiently recovered to climb on your own. Follow me."

Mary and her mother began climbing the ladder. As they moved up the ladder the lights behind them turned off and the lights above came on section by section. Up and up they climbed until Mary's legs and arms were aching.

"I can't climb any more," Mary cried.

Mary's mother paused in her climb and said, "Rest a minute, then continue climbing. I have to get to the control room and start the launch sequence. I will return for you if you cannot make it to the top."

Mary clung desperately to the ladder. Her knees were shaking and her arms felt like lead weights. She was cold and scratched from the run through the forest.

"If this is a bad dream I hope I wake up soon," she said aloud, her voice echoing in the large space.

She could no longer hear her mother climbing and thought, *Mother must have made it to the top. It can't be that much farther. I have to go on.*

She gritted her teeth and began climbing again. The ladder seemed to go on forever.

Then she climbed into a compartment that was very odd. It was round just like the other rooms but it had chairs attached to the wall in rows all the way around the space. Some of the chairs were upside down. *I wonder how you sit in those*, she thought.

The ladder continued up through the center of the room and through the ceiling. She could hear rumbling noises below and the room started vibrating. Frightened, she began climbing again. Mary climbed on and on until lost count of the rooms she gone through. They all seemed topsy-turvy with chairs and tables in strange positions.

This has got to be the worst bad dream I have ever had! She thought.

When she finally got to the top of the ladder she found her mother lying on her back in a chair facing a bewildering bank of lights, buttons and gauges. Mary thought it looked just like a picture of a cockpit she had seen in a book about airplanes, except there was no window in front of her mother, just the biggest TV screen Mary had ever seen. At the moment the screen was blank.

“Good, you are here”, Mary’s mother said as she got out of the chair. “Please sit in this chair and I will strap you in.”

Mary climbed into the chair and her mother pulled straps tightly around her. Soon she was strapped in the chair so tightly that she was unable to move at all.

“Why are you doing this and what is going on, Mother?” Mary asked.

“I don’t have time to explain now. Remain quiet and I will tell you when you are safe.”

Mary’s mother climbed back into her chair just as the screen in front of her lit up and a series of characters scrolled down. Mary thought they looked like a mixed up alphabet. Then the vibration became stronger and a roar started at the bottom of the cylinder and Mary felt the room moving. It started out feeling like an elevator that was moving up slowly but soon she felt a lot of pressure pushing her down into her seat as they moved faster and faster. The pressure became so bad that Mary thought she would soon be unable to breathe. Her arms felt like lead. She was completely unable to move.

Just as she thought she couldn’t stand it anymore, the pressure began to lessen, and then was completely gone. Mary breathed a sigh of relief. She relaxed in the chair and appreciated the simple ability to breathe without a struggle. She still could not move because she was strapped in so tightly. She could turn her head and she looked at her mother who was busily pushing buttons and checking the screen.

"Mother, please tell me what is happening," pleaded Mary.

"Not now, Mary, I will explain later. You need to be quiet. I know that takeoff was frightening, but this next step will be worse. Do not be afraid. You will feel very strange. If you try to relax it will not be as bad. Do not try to talk. It will not last long."

Mary opened her mouth to ask another question but she was unable to form the words. Her entire body felt as if she was being stretched and melted. The room around her seemed to twist and buckle. Lights flickered and floated. Someone was screaming. The TV in front of her appeared to flow down the wall. Visions of Mary's classmates at school floated in the air in front of her screaming, "Red head, red head, dead red head!"

Am I dying? She wondered. Then everything went black.

Slowly Mary began to awaken but she was afraid to open her eyes.

Oh, please let me be in my bed at home, she thought.

When she finally opened her eyes she was still in the strange room and she was still strapped in the chair.

At least my body isn't melted and lying in a pool in the floor.

Mary strained against the straps. They were becoming very uncomfortable. She glanced over at her mother and finally got up the courage to say, "Please loosen the straps. They are hurting me."

Her mother looked over at her and said, "I see you have regained consciousness. I have to finish this sequence. I will attend to you in a moment."

Mary felt very dispirited. She had just gone through the most frightening thing in her life and yet she received no comfort from her mother. She sighed and tried to get comfortable until her mother could release her. Then she noticed something very unusual. A tear that had slipped from her eye was floating in front of her face.

"Mother, a tiny drop of water is floating in front of me!" Mary exclaimed.

Her mother somewhat distractedly replied "We have traveled far from Earth. There is no gravity here. Now please remain quiet while I finish."

"Finish what?" Mary asked.

"I have to check the coordinates in the guidance system and make sure it is properly calibrated. One tiny miscalculation could cause us to be millions of light years off course."

Mary tried to comprehend what her mother had said but she was very confused. A few minutes later her mother, apparently finished with her work, unstrapped her safety harness and floated over to Mary. "Mary, be careful when I take the straps off. It may take a while but you will learn how to move about in zero gravity."

"Mother, please tell me what has happened," Mary pleaded. "I don't understand."

Mary's mother paused a moment and said "I will explain soon. You will understand."

Mary resigned herself to waiting for answers to her questions but right now she had a more pressing problem. She couldn't keep her gown from floating up. Her mother noticed the problem and floated to a cabinet on the wall and located a set of clothes for Mary. "How did you know to have clothes here for me?" Mary asked.

"We always had supplies and clothing ready for escape at a moment's notice. We had to be prepared. You must be protected. Now please get dressed and I will prepare nourishment for you."

Mary discovered that dressing in zero gravity was difficult. She kept bouncing off the walls and her clothes kept drifting away. It was a struggle but somehow she managed to get dressed.

Eating without gravity was a challenge as well. The liquid food was in plastic tubes. The red one was tomato soup. She didn't know what the blue one was but it tasted very good. There were also little bite-size cubes. The white ones were bread and the yellow ones were cheeses. She discovered that she was hungry and quickly mastered the art of drinking from the plastic tube and popping the cubes into her mouth. She made a game of floating the cubes in front of her and then catching them in her mouth.

She was having such a good time that she almost forgot where she was and the events of the morning. Then she remembered that she had not seen her father. "Mother, where is Father?" she asked.

"Father will not be joining us," was mother's reply.

"Why?" Mary asked, puzzled by mother's answer.

"He stayed behind to make sure we escaped and no one would follow us," she answered.

"Will he be OK?"

"It is not important. What is important is that you are safe."

"Why is it so important that I am safe?"

"I can see you will not rest until you understand your situation. Please follow me into the control room. It is time you met your true mother."

Mary followed her into the control room and watched as her mother placed a tiny cassette into a slot in the bottom of the viewing screen. In a few moments a woman's face appeared on the screen. Mary gasped as she realized it was the face of the beautiful woman in her dreams. Then the woman began to speak.

"My beloved child, how do I begin to explain why I have allowed you be taken away from me? Believe me when I say there is no other way to keep you safe. Your life is more important than my torment at your leaving me. You are the hope and the future of Ayri. Nothing or no one must stand in the way of keeping you safe. I only hope that you will find it in your heart to forgive me when you have been told the entire story. I love you. I always have and I always will."

Tears began to flow when Mary heard her true mother's words. She looked expectantly at the screen, hoping to hear more, but the image faded and the screen went blank. "Is there more? Why did it stop?" Mary screamed, reaching blindly for the control panel. It was too much to have only a brief glimpse of the person she knew in her heart was her true mother and to feel the love her mother managed to put in to the short message. She wanted and begged to hear more, only to have her hopes dashed.

"Mary, calm down and listen to me. Your true mother didn't have much time to record the message. If we were to succeed in getting you away from Ayri, we had to move quickly. The Bahadin were attacking the royal residence. We barely made our escape."

Mary turned away from the screen and looked at the person she had believed to be her mother, as if she had never seen her before. She didn't know what to say or believe. "Who are you?'

"I am X'akara. X'orige and I were your mother's servants. She entrusted us with your care and protection until it was safe to return home."

"X'orige? Who is that," Mary asked.

"X'orige was the one you called father."

"You said he would not be joining us." Mary said, "What will happen to him?"

"X'orige stayed behind to destroy the dwelling we inhabited on Earth. He did this to make the Bahadin think that you were killed to avoid being captured."

"Is he...do you think he is dead?" Mary managed to ask as tears welled up in her eyes. Though he had never been the kind and loving father she wanted, he was the only father she had known.

"Mary, X'orige was not alive in the sense that you are alive. He is a CAMCIA. A **C**omputer **A**ctivated **M**achine **C**apable of **I**ndependent **A**ctions. I am also a CAMCIA. Your true mother wanted you to be protected from whatever dangers that you might encounter and instructed us not to inform any living being or machine where we were going, not even herself. She chose CAMCIA's to care for you because a human could possibly betray you, become sick or die. You were too young to remember Ayri or your family so your true mother instructed us that you not to be told of your origins so you could not endanger yourself inadvertently.

We chose Earth for your hiding place because it was many light years from Ayri and had a similar ecological system. The humans inhabiting earth were biologically similar to the people of Ayri. When we were close to Earth we transitioned out of hypervelocity and began observing the planet and its inhabitants closely. X'orige and I chose an area with a moderate climate that was sparsely inhabited and after we had deciphered the language and customs we landed in a remote area and built the tunnel to hide our ship. Judging from the local inhabitants we decided that we would not arouse suspicion if we posed as a family."

Mary sat back in the chair. She felt so very tired and alone. In one day her entire world had drastically changed. Still she could not rest until she knew why this had happened. "Mother…ah X'akara," Mary stammered, "What am I to call you now?"

"You should call me X'akara. There is no need to continue the ruse at this time."

"Is there another recording of my Mother? Mary asked.

"There are no more recordings, but I will tell you of your home and your family's history. It is a long story, but we have a long time. Even traveling at hypervelocity it will take 2 years to travel to the transition point. There are many things you will need to learn while we are on this voyage."

"Are we going to my mother's home?"

"We will not return to Ayri at this time. We will first go to Tiros a sparsely inhabited planet where your mother has placed a secret signal station. We will check for messages from her. If there is no signal from her we will send a coded message. Then we will wait for a reply but you do not need to worry about that now. We have a very long voyage ahead of us."

Mary nodded her understanding and asked, "What do I need to do now?"

X'akara assessed Mary's condition and determined that she was exhausted by her ordeal and said, "Now you need to rest for a while. It has been a long day and you need to keep up your strength. I will show you where you are to sleep."

Mary followed X'akara out of the control room through the dining area and into the next room. She admired the smooth way X'akara moved about in the ship and tried to imitate her movements. Mary wasn't as graceful, but she did succeed in keeping up with X'akara.

The arrangement of the furniture that was so puzzling when she was climbing the ladder now made perfect sense in the zero gravity of space.

"This is the sleeping chamber," X'akara said as she opened one of the compartments that lined the walls. She reached inside and pulled out a bed covered with a blanket and webbing.

"What's this stuff for?" Mary asked, examining the webbing.

X'akara explained, "If you are not secured in the webbing you will float about the compartment and you could possibly get hurt."

"Oh," Mary said as she climbed into the bed.

X'akara helped Mary secure the webbing. Mary was sure she wouldn't be able to fall asleep with so much on her mind. As she floated just above the bunk she thought about the day's events. It was now clear why she had received no affection from her "parents". It didn't make the past hurts go away but she was beginning to understand the reason they were so cold.

Then Mary thought about the beautiful woman who had held her in her dreams so many nights. To think she was really her mother and loved her made Mary feel warm inside, and it was with these thoughts that she fell asleep. She was already dreaming before X'akara slipped from the room. X'akara, of course, being a robot needed no sleep. She kept watch over the ship while Mary slept.

Chapter 3

Meanwhile back on earth a single shuttle blasts off and limps toward an enormous ship hidden behind Earth's moon. Aboard are the few remaining Bahadin CAMCIA soldiers that were sent to capture Mary. The shuttle is severely damaged and is barely able to make it to the ship and into the docking bay. When the shuttle is secured the Lead CAMCIA soldier climbs out and walks to the end of the docking bay and up three levels to the control room door. The artificial gravity of the ship is less than the gravity on the planet below, and he moves awkwardly until his system adjusts to the lower gravity. When the adjustment is complete he is able to move with the smooth motion of a CAMCIA. He places his hand on the identification pad and the door slides open. He steps inside and walks over to the main control area and stands near the Commander's chair, which is facing the control panel. The soldier waits to be acknowledged.

The Chair swivels around to reveal Voltrod, Commander of the Bahadin Warship Falconoid. His small beady eyes radiate his anger as he smoothes the long whiskers on either side of his snout with his paw-like hands. The humanoid shape of the CAMCIA is repulsive to the commander but he knows his anger is lost on the machine. "Report CAMCIA," he shouts in frustration.

The soldier snaps to attention and says, "Commander Voltrod, Lead CAMCIA 0502-10 reporting, sir."

"I assume that since you do not have the child with you that you have failed to capture her," Voltrod says, his anger barely contained. "How could one small child have eluded the finest CAMCIA soldiers in the universe?"

"Sir, we believe the child was killed in an explosion that destroyed the dwelling."

"And, just how did you come by this conclusion?" Voltrod snarls, his patience growing thin.

"Sir, when we landed we had a life form reading emanating from the dwelling. We were in the process of deploying soldiers to the dwelling when we came under heavy fire. All of our shuttles but one were totally destroyed before we could eliminate the sniper. We proceeded to enter the dwelling. Moments after the troops entered the dwelling it was totally destroyed by a massive explosion that was probably triggered by a motion detector. A check of the life-form indicator revealed no viable life form in the immediate area. I ordered the remaining soldiers to retrieve the damaged CAMCIA and board the shuttle. We then returned to the ship."

"Was there any indication of a launch in the area?" Voltrod asked.

"We were not aware of any launch, however much of our equipment was damaged or destroyed in the attack," the soldier answered.

"Report on the damage." Voltrod ordered.

"Six shuttles and thirty six CAMCIA's were destroyed. There are five CAMCIA's damaged but repairable."

"If you have nothing else to report you are dismissed," Voltrod growled.

The Lead CAMCIA bowed to Voltrod turned and left the control room.

Voltrod was not convinced that the child was destroyed. He was certain it would not be that easy. He was troubled by the destruction of CAMCIA's and equipment as well. The high command would not look favorably on the amount of equipment they had lost and he knew that failure to complete the assignment would not be tolerated. A small lapse in judgement could lead to demotion; defeat on this scale would be worse, much worse. He had brought about his own advancement by casting doubt on his commander's leadership capabilities. He could easily be the next to lose at this game.

He drummed his fingers on the arm of his chair as he considered his alternatives. "Send for L'abart," he ordered.

A few minutes later L'abart sauntered into the control room. He was a small, weasel faced humanoid man but he walked with the swagger of a giant, as he believed himself to be indispensable.

"You called, Voltrod?" he asked with a smirk.

Voltrod could barely contain his revulsion, as he faced L'abart. "The shuttle has just returned from the planet. They went to the location you specified and detected a dwelling. The CAMCIA soldiers report that they encountered heavy resistance when they approached the habitation. As they entered the building an explosion destroyed it. They think the child was caught in the blast and destroyed. I think the explosion may have been a diversion and that the child has escaped. What do you sense? Is the child dead?"

L'abart hesitated and feigned concentration as he placed his fingers on his brow and closed his eyes. He projected his thoughts toward the child "Where are you?"

At that moment, somewhere in space, Mary was jolted out of a deep sleep. She opened her eyes and looked around. No one was there. "I must be dreaming", she thought as she slipped back into a deep sleep.

L'abart didn't need to concentrate to feel her power. He could tell she was no longer close and that she was rapidly moving further and further away but still her strength was amazing. *If she ever harnesses that awesome* *power...*He shivered, afraid to finish the thought. He needed time to compose his answer. Voltrod was not going to like what he had to say.

L'abart knew Voltrod despised him and the feeling was mutual but L'abart also knew he had to keep the uneasy alliance with him. They both wanted the same thing, but for different reasons.

Voltrod was ordered to capture Mary because the Bahadin wanted to use her as a pawn in the war against Ayri. The war had been going on much too long. The Bahadin thought of themselves as the great conquerors and controlled many planets. They had never been defeated but now they were fighting a losing battle against a small planet they should have conquered easily. The people of Ayri were not skilled in warfare when the Bahadin first attacked but they learned quickly. The Bahadin believed Ayri would stop resisting if Mary were dead or captured.

L'abart, on the other hand wanted her dead because he desired the throne of Ayri. He was a distant relative of the royal family of Ayri. He knew he didn't have a chance at the power he longed for unless he could somehow destroy the royal family.

"It's stupid to have a woman ruler," he told himself the day he set out to betray his planet. "I would be a much better ruler!"

He went to the Bahadin and offered his services in return for a promise that he would be appointed governor-general when Ayri was conquered. Of course when he was governor-general he would turn on the Bahadin. He considered them to be stupid brutes that he could easily manipulate with his powers. He had no loyalties except to himself.

He opened his eyes and sighed, "Alas, you are right. The child lives, though she is no longer on this planet."

"Where is she?" Voltrod asked.

L'abart considered his answer for a moment. "She is moving away at a high rate. I think she must be in a ship traveling at hypervelocity."

"Can you at least say which direction she is traveling?" Voltrod shouted banging his fist on the arm of the chair.

"My dear Voltrod, there is no need to shout. I can not, as you well know, determine the exact location of a person traveling at hypervelocity, but I believe she is headed in the general direction of Ayri." L'abart answered as if he were speaking to a child who had asked a foolish question.

Voltrod, angered at the pompous little man, turned away and began giving orders for the ship to be prepared to jump to hypervelocity. He gave the pilot the coordinates for Ayri and turning back to L'abart he sneered, "I suggest that you return to your cabin and prepare for hypervelocity, unless you would enjoy sharing your agony during the jump to hypervelocity with the crew."

The Bahadin prided themselves on their ability to withstand the transition to hypervelocity without losing consciousness. The people of Ayri were considered weaklings because they suffered a great deal of discomfort during the jump.

L'abart, stormed back to his cabin. *When I take over I will get even with that detestable Bahadin!* He thought to himself.

Chapter 4

Mary awoke slowly from a wonderful dream about the beautiful red haired lady that she now knew was her true mother. A light over her bed was blinking and there was a beeping coming from a speaker near her head. At first she was disoriented and confused, but then she remembered where she was.

"An alarm clock! Even on a space ship I have to have an alarm clock!" she said as she released the webbing that held her in the bunk and floated into the dining area.

X'akara turned around from the wall unit where she was busy heating a food packet. "Good morning. I trust you rested well."

"Good morning, I slept very well, thank you." Mary answered automatically. It was the same greeting that she had heard every morning for as long as she could remember but it certainly seemed different today.

"I have worked out a training schedule for you. We will begin after you have had your morning nourishment."

Mary opened the end of the food packet and began eating her morning meal. It tasted remarkably good but she couldn't help but wonder what it was.

"X'akara," Mary said holding the packet up to see if there was any markings to indicate what type of food she was eating, "what is this stuff?"

"It is maoteal, a cereal grain that is very nutritious. It is best when heated with a little water and a sweetener. When it is packaged in an airtight container it retains its nutrients and remains fresh for many years. It is a staple food source on Ayri. You are fortunate that there are many foods from Ayri in our ship stores. You will have time to become accustomed to your native foods during our journey. Now, if you are finished with your morning food we will begin your training."

Mary followed X'akara through the sleeping quarters into a large room that had many compartments lining the walls. X'akara opened one of the panels and pulled out a device that had a seat with a safety harness and pedals. Along the top there were a series of levers and handles. X'akara buckled Mary into the machine and clamped the pedals on her feet.

"This is an exercise machine. Because we have no artificial gravity on this ship it is necessary that you exercise everyday to keep your muscles from deteriorating. First the machine will test your strength and endurance. Then it will determine the amount of exercise you will need. Begin pedaling now. When you can no longer pedal, press the red button. Then start the next segment by pushing the handlebars as far in front of you as you can and then pull them back as far as you can. When you can no longer move the bars, press the red button again."

Mary began pedaling. The pedals gradually became harder and harder to move. When she reached the point that she couldn't make the pedals move she pressed the red button. After resting for a moment she pushed the handlebars forward. They moved easily at first but with each push forward they became more difficult to move. Soon she was unable to move the bars at all and she pushed the red button.

"You may rest while the machine calculates your exercise program. It will calculate the amount of exertion you have already expended and will reduce the amount of exercise for today. When the green light comes on press it to begin. The machine will tell you what to do." X'akara explained. "I will be back when you finish."

X'akara floated out of the exercise room and Mary began her exercises. The machine kept her busy, changing from pedals to handlebars and then both at the same time. While she worked the machine played a catchy little song. It seemed more like a game than work to Mary. She was almost sad when the machine informed her that her workout was complete for today.

X'akara came back a few seconds after Mary was finished. She had a cool drink for Mary. "You must drink plenty of fluids when you exercise." She said.

Mary needed no encouragement. She found she was very thirsty.

"Now, Mary, we need to go to the study area and begin learning Versal Basic. It is the common language of our galaxy. You will need to know it when we reach our destination. You already know Ayria the language of your home planet."

"I do?" Mary interrupted, "I don't remember learning a new language."

"While you were on Earth you received sleep suggestion language training at night. The memory was suppressed during your waking hours by repression therapy. You would only remember the language when triggered by a key sentence."

"What is the sentence? Will I remember all at once?" Mary asked.

"You have already heard the key sentence. It was the first words your mother spoke to you on the tape. Did you not wonder how you understood her?" X'akara questioned.

When Mary thought about it she realized that her mother's words were not English, but she did understand. "Can't we do that sleep thing for this new language?" Mary asked, obviously trying to get out of studying.

"Sleep suggestion language training is not appropriate this time. It would take a very long time and you need to study to keep your mind occupied. It is not difficult to learn Versal Basic." X'akara explained.

Mary followed X'akara to the other side of the training room where a desk was concealed behind another door. A computer monitor and keyboard were mounted to the desk. X'akara pulled a chair from under the desk.

"The chair is connected by a track to the floor and has a seat belt to keep you from floating away from the desk. I have programmed the computer to teach Versal Basic to you using the alphabet you learned on Earth. You should have no trouble following the instructions. When you have completed the first assignment you will have free time until lunch. After lunch you will return to the computer to begin learning the Versal alphabet and the alphabet of Ayri. When you complete your lessons correctly you will have leisure time until your evening meal. I have not scheduled any other classes at this time."

Mary sighed and slipped into the chair. She thought being on a space ship would have been a lot more fun that this. She wisely did not share her feelings with X'akara, who wouldn't have understood at all.

Mary worked diligently at the computer and had to admit the program made learning a new language interesting. She lost track of the time and was surprised when the computer signaled that she had successfully completed the first lesson.

That wasn't so bad she thought as she unbuckled the seat belt and pushed off the chair a little too hard and found herself flying toward the wall. At the last moment she was able to turn and land on her feet. She pushed off the wall with a little less force and floated slowly toward the middle of the room. *Oops,* she thought, *How am I going to get back to the desk?*

Eventually she floated close enough to grab the ladder. *This is going to take some practice,* she thought as she pushed off the ladder and floated to the desk.

I'm not going give up!

Eventually she found that if she pushed just right she could go all the way across the room without stopping. Then she tried to flip around mid way, land on her feet and push herself back across the room. Of course she had to be careful not to hit the ladder in the center of the room. As she became better at judging the distances she taped paper targets around the room and made up more complicated moves. She was so busy playing she didn't notice X'akara watching from the door.

"It is time for your lunch."

When X'akara spoke it startled Mary and she missed the third rung of the ladder and banged her head. X'akara moved quickly to Mary's side and said "Mary, are you injured?"

"Oh my head," Mary groaned "That hurt."

At that exact moment, somewhere far, far away a young boy abruptly dropped his training module and grabbed his head. "Oh my head," he groaned, "That hurt." His older brother alarmed by the pained expression said, "L'amie, what is wrong?"

"It feels like something hit me in the head."

L'reg examined his brother's head but could not see any damage. "Do you want me to send for the physician?" he asked.

"No it is not bad. It feels better now. I wonder if it was"

His brother quickly placed his hand over L'amie's mouth. "Don't say it. Don't even think it. It is much too dangerous."

X'akara examined Mary's head and looked into her eyes. "I believe you will have a small bruise but I see no significant damage. You must try to be more careful. I think you would have more success if you would watch where you are going."

Mary knew X'akara would never understand playing or having fun. It didn't hurt her feelings as much now that Mary knew that X'akara was a CAMCIA, but she really wished she had someone to play with.

Mary was quite sure that it would be a long boring voyage but time passed much quicker than Mary thought it would. X'akara made sure Mary stayed busy studying and exercising. Mary occupied her free time exploring the ship and playing games she invented.

Soon Mary became so proficient at speaking Versal Basic and Ayria that X'akara proclaimed that they would no longer communicate in English.

Mary completed all the study programs on the computer shortly before her eleventh birthday. She knew it was her birthday because X'akara had written a complicated computer program to determine the date in Earth days factoring in the time inconsistencies caused by traveling in hypervelocity.

Mary was looking forward to her birthday because, for the first time in her life she was going to have a birthday party. On Earth she had never received a gift or a party simply because X'akara and "X'orige didn't know about the tradition.

When Mary told X'akara about birthday presents and parties X'akara agreed to prepare a special treat for Mary.

"Here Mary, I have prepared a nutritious birthday cake for you," X'akara said and handed Mary a plastic tube with maoteal inside.

Mary thought it was her usual breakfast cereal until she tasted it. X'akara had added extra sweeteners to it and another substance that Mary couldn't identify. It tasted different but good. It wasn't a cake but Mary loved it anyway. At least X'akara had tried to make it special.

Then Mary got another surprise. For Mary's birthday present X'akara loaded the training module from the ship's shuttle on Mary's computer. Mary thought it was a game and became obsessed with mastering the simulation. She spent almost all of her free time working on the training module.

One day after many long sessions on the computer Mary called X'akara into the study room.

"X'akara, look. I have passed the landing sequence test. I didn't crash this time!" Mary exclaimed, "This is a great game, I love it!"

"Mary, this is not a game. This is the actual training module for the shuttle. When you have finished all the test simulations you will be a certified shuttle pilot."

Mary was amazed and excited and started working even harder to complete the training.

Chapter 5

One night X'akara came to Mary and said, "It is time you learned the history of your home and your family but I must warn you never to reveal who you are until we are safely back with your parents on Ayri."

It was what Mary had been waiting to hear. She had asked repeatedly during the voyage but X'akara would only say, "when it is time".

As Mary settled into a comfortable position X'akara began the story.

"Long ago the planet that is now known as Ayri was settled by nomadic migrants who had been cast out by their home planet because of their unusual powers. They wandered the galaxy for many years until they found a beautiful uninhabited planet they named Ayri.

After being confined to the small rag-tag collection of space ships for so long Ayri seemed like paradise. The sky was a brilliant blue and the water that flowed in the many rivers and streams were clean and pure. There were huge forests of trees that were hundreds of feet high as well as valleys with tall grasses and mountains that reached for the sky.

They set about making the planet their home. They constructed homes and beautiful cities. They wanted their planet to be unpolluted and to protect the wonderful home they had found.

They knew they had to have strong leadership to keep from having the chaos they had endured on the planet they left behind. They decided to have a competition among the families to determine who should lead them.

The competition included many types of challenges including tests of physical strength and intelligence. The most important test was telepathic energy. In a world where everyone had some telepathic powers it was extremely important for their leader to be very strong telepathically. The trials went on for many months and in the end one person was clearly the best suited for the position of Sovereign of Ayri. She was L'arpell and she was your ancestor."

Mary's eyes grew big and round as she heard X'akara's words. "My ancestor was the first ruler of Ayri! Wow! You mean I'm related to somebody important. I can't believe it. All my life I have felt like an outsider, as if I didn't matter."

X'akara didn't understand Mary's excitement and she couldn't comprehend the emotions Mary had experienced so she waited until Mary was quiet and continued with her narrative.

"Yes, your ancestor L'arpell was the first ruler of Ayri. She ruled with compassion and intelligence. Under her direction Ayri prospered and the people were happy. The rule of the planet was passed down to L'arpell's daughter, L'estele, when she became of age. And so it has been through the ages. Each ruler has passed the reign to her first born daughter until the present day. There has always been a direct female descendent to inherit the title. With each successive age the telepathic power of the female ruler has increased, but each ruler was a good and noble leader who helped her people thrive.

Ayri had good relations with the inhabitants of nearby planets and they traded frequently with Ayri. The people of Ayri prospered and reached outward with their trade ships. Then Ayri ships encountered the Bahadin.

The Bahadin were from an aggressive warrior planet on the outskirts of the next galaxy. Their leaders valued conquest above all other things. They had been systematically conquering and destroying all the inhabited planets they discovered. They would then take any survivors they found and use them as slave labor. The slaves were forced to serve them on wretched and dangerous planets, mining for ore and doing other degrading things that the Bahadin considered beneath them.

The Bahadin captured one of Ayri's trade ships and tortured the crew when they refused to reveal the location of Ayri. Everyone on Ayri could feel the pain and suffering of the crew as they died. It was the darkest day Ayri had ever known.

The people of Ayri vowed to protect their home planet and its inhabitants. To that end an alliance with the surrounding planets was formed. Each world worked frantically to build their defenses.

When the Bahadin finally attacked the outermost planet, Zuplo they expected no resistance. They were caught off guard. The people of Zuplo fought courageously and were successful in keeping the Bahadin at bay. The ships from Ayri arrived in time to help complete the victory. The Bahadin had never before suffered defeat. The remnants of their attack wing struggled back to Bahadin in disgrace.

When he heard of the defeat at Zuplo the Bahadin ruler, Uglure the Magnificent was furious. He called the surviving Wing Commander into his chambers. 'How can it be that you were defeated?' he shouted.

The Wing Commander knew he had to come up with someone or something to blame for his degrading defeat. Commanders who failed didn't survive long. He claimed Ayri caused his defeat. He told Uglure that Ayri had instigated the build up of weapons and had made alliances with the other planets in order to attack Bahadin. Uglure believed his story, but it didn't save the Wing Commander. Uglure had him executed.

Based on the Wing Commander's story the Bahadin concentrated all their war efforts on Ayri. They sent a much larger force to attack Ayri. They encountered resistance from the other planets, especially Zuplo on their way to Ayri and fierce fighting at Ayri. They were unable to gain a foothold in Ayri. They tried landing spies on the planet but each one was quickly detected and captured. It was difficult to penetrate a planet where all the inhabitants were telepathic. The Bahadin didn't understand how the people were always able to spot an intruder.

One thing they understood was that the Sovereign was beloved by the people and she had no female heir. They couldn't comprehend the concept of a female ruler. Females on their planets were considered weaklings and were not treated much better than slaves. Nethertheless they knew that the people of Ayri believed as long as there was a direct female descendent of L'arpell the planet could not fall. The Bahadin concluded that if they could capture this female Sovereign and hold her hostage the people would bow down. If they could prevent the Sovereign from giving birth to a female child the long reign of the family of L'arpell would come to an end and with it the hopes of the people of Ayri.

The Sovereign had spies of her own and it was though these spies that she learned of the plot. She increased the security around the royal residence and called on her loyal subjects to help her devise a plan to keep her secret. She knew the Bahadin would soon discover that she was expecting a child. If they thought the child was a girl they would increase their efforts to capture her. The plan was to announce that she was expecting a boy child. What she hoped to keep secret was that she was expecting twins, one of whom was indeed a boy but the other was the long awaited Heir Apparent Female. She knew she would have to protect the female child and the only way she could protect her would be to send her far away from the war. It was a chance she was willing to take but it broke her heart to think of her beautiful child being taken away.

"So Mary, your mother chose X'orige and me to care for you and keep you safe from harm."

The Bahadin concentrated their attack on the capital city of Merald and managed to penetrate the shield. They were advancing on the royal residence as we carried you to the ship.

Mary was speechless. She had always thought of herself as being an intimidated, insignificant little girl. Now she was being told she was a princess. The funny thing was, she didn't feel different. *What does a princess feel like anyway?* She wondered.

"Wait a minute," Mary said suddenly remembering something X'akara had said, "Did you say my mother was expecting twins? Does that mean I have a brother, a twin brother?"

"Yes, Mary you have a twin brother," X'akara answered "As well as an older brother."

"Two brothers! What are their names, do you know? And my mother and father, what are their names? And is my name really Mary?"

"Your older brother is L'reg, your twin is L'amie," X'akara answered as soon as Mary paused for breath, "Your mother is The Sovereign L'alie, your father Consort L'sasle, and you are The Sovereign Heir Apparent L'demi."

Mary was overwhelmed by it all. All she could say was "The Sovereign Heir Apparent L'demi, what a mouth full."

"I am sorry, I do not understand, what could be filling your mouth?" X'akara asked.

"I mean my name is very long. Not at all like Mary."

"Of course it a lofty title, but until we can reach the safety of your home I will continue to call you Mary."

Mary thought for a minute and then said, "Alright, I'm used to Mary anyway. Besides exactly what does it mean, The Sovereign Heir Apparent L'demi?"

"It means that you are the future ruler of Ayri." X'akara answered.

"How can I rule a planet, I'm only a kid. I don't know anything about ruling a planet." Mary cried out.

"You will learn, as your mother learned, as her mother before her learned." X'akara answered.

Mary thought it was maddening how unconcerned X'akara could be about something so overpowering as the idea of ruling an entire planet could be.

"And didn't you say all these people are telepathic? I don't stand a chance. They will all know I'm not telepathic and kick me out."

"Do not concern yourself with the details at this time, Mary. You will have time to learn the skills to govern. You have not learned to use your telepathy on Earth and I am unable to determine your telepathic ability. When you are returned to Ayri, you will have time to learn that as well. There has never been a ruler of Ayri who did not possess telepathy." X'akara answered in the same monotone she used to instruct Mary in the proper way to brush her teeth.

Mary wanted to stomp and shout and slam a door. Unfortunately it is impossible to stomp in space and there were no doors to slam, so she settled for bouncing around the exercise room screaming and shouting at the top of her lungs. It did help to blow off some steam. And in the end Mary went to bed totally exhausted.

Chapter 6

The whoop of the emergency signal startled Mary out of a sound sleep. The ship was shaking, vibrating and a loud roar replaced the usual background hum of the engines.

As she quickly unbuckled the sleep net, Mary said, "Why does everything happen when I am asleep?"

She made her way to the control room where X'akara was busy working at the controls.

"What's going on," Mary shouted over the loud cry of the emergency alarm.

X'akara didn't take her attention away from the controls when she answered, "We have a major malfunction and may have to abandon ship. I have been unable to determine the amount of damage. Strap yourself in your seat, tightly."

Mary moved to the chair and began to buckle the straps. Her hands were shaking as she pulled the belt tight.

"What is wrong with the ship?" Mary asked.

"According to the instruments we have a failure of the ship's hull in the engine compartment. I have sealed the engine compartment but I will have to bring the ship out of hypervelocity, if possible, before I can determine the full extent of the damage. You may feel a little disoriented as we make the transition to normal speed."

As the ship folded into normal space Mary lost consciousness. It did not seem as bad as the jump into hypervelocity had been. *I must be getting used to this space travel,* she thought as she regained her senses and looked around.

X'akara released her harness and glided across the compartment. "Mary, I am going outside to survey the damage to the engine compartment hull and attempt to make the repairs. While I am outside you will wait in the shuttle. I will show you how to get in the shuttle. Do not leave the shuttle until I can determine the extent of the damage. If the alarm sounds again you must activate the shuttle and disconnect from the ship. According to the readout there is a class 3 planet within the shuttle's range. Go there.

"Without you?" Mary asked.

"Affirmative."

Mary followed X'akara to the shuttle bay and climbed inside. It was the first time she had been in the actual shuttle. She immediately noticed the similarity to the training screen on her computer.

"This gadget is exactly like the controls on the simulator." Mary said.

It was exciting to see the real thing but she was apprehensive. Mary realized that playing with a computer simulation was different from the real thing. As much as she wanted to try flying the shuttle she didn't want to do it the first time alone.

After what seemed like several hours of waiting Mary was a nervous wreck. "What is X'akara doing?" she agonized. Why doesn't she let me know? She tried to imagine what X'akara could be doing and strained to hear any sign that she might be returning. Just when she thought she couldn't stand it any longer, X'akara opened the shuttle door. Mary was limp with relief that X'akara was back.

"There is extensive damage that will take a great deal of time to repair. You can not remain here while I make the repairs."

"Why not?" Mary asked.

"The oxygen generators are damaged and are not functioning properly. Do not waste any time preparing to leave. You have only a few minutes to pack some food and clothing before your breathing will become difficult. When you have gathered your things take the shuttle to the class 3 planet I identified on the navigational screen earlier. I will notify you as soon as it is safe for you to return," X'akara instructed as Mary climbed from the shuttle.

Mary was still quite shaky after the long anxious wait in the shuttle. She looked at X'akara in surprise. "What!" she exclaimed, "You want me to take the shuttle to the planet? By myself? You can't be serious!"

"Mary, you have completed your training on the simulator with a 98.365% competency rating." X'akara answered, "You are a certified shuttle pilot."

"But, I never tried the real thing. Why can't you take me to the planet and then come back and repair the ship?"

"The ship is within the outer gravitation pull of the planet. I only have a short time to complete the engine repairs before the ship reaches the upper atmosphere of the planet. If I can not get the engines repaired and in operation before this happens the ship will be pulled into the atmosphere where it will burn as it crashes into the planet. There is not sufficient time to take you to the planet and return to the ship." X'akara answered in her usual unemotional tone.

Mary was overwhelmed by her fears, not only of flying the shuttle but being alone on the surface of the planet. It was almost more than she could stand.

X'akara, totally unaware of Mary's plight, continued with her instructions, "The sensors indicate that the mean temperature on the planet is at the upper range for humans, so you will only need a minimum of clothing. There is packaged food in the dining area. Take as much as you can carry in one trip to the shuttle. There is a food tester in the shuttle that will indicate which of the natural foods on the planet are editable. Do not drink or eat anything until you test it." With that comment X'akara turned and pulled herself toward the engine compartment.

Mary was unable to move, immobilized by her fear. X'akara turned as she left the compartment. "Mary, there is not much oxygen left, begin loading the shuttle," X'akara said using the tone of voice that Mary had been trained to obey without question.

Mary moved to comply with X'akara's command, automatically. She didn't stop to analyze her feelings until later.

Mary slid a large bundle of food containers from under the counter in the dining area and pushed it ahead of her as she floated back to the shuttle. She unlatched the door and pushed the food into the storage compartment. Then she pulled the door shut and secured it. She settled herself in the pilot seat, buckled her harness securely, took a deep breath and tried to calm down. When she pushed the button to start the shuttle the slight rumble of the engine reassured her. She checked the instruments to make sure the shuttle was functioning correctly and the airtight shuttle door was sealed. Then she pressed the switch that opened the bay door.

Mary pressed the communication switch and said, "X'akara, this is Mary, I am proceeding to undock the shuttle."

"Mary: proceed with flight. No further communications will be necessary until you have landed on the surface."

Mary pulled the release pin and eased the shuttle out of the bay. Mary noted that X'akara had programmed the navigation computer to lock on to the planet and enter the atmosphere at the correct angle. Now all Mary had to do was initiate the program and sit back until the shuttle was just above the surface of the planet. Then would come the real test of her training. Mary willed her hand to stop shaking as she touched the computer screen. The engines barely made a sound as the shuttle sped toward the planet.

Mary knew that the shuttle had to enter the atmosphere at just the right angle. Too shallow an angle and the shuttle would bounce off the atmosphere. Too steep and the shuttle would gain too much speed and the friction would cause the ship to burn. To Mary's relief the shuttle entered smoothly with hardly any friction.

Mary had been able to relax a little during the brief flight to the planet, but now she was becoming nervous again. As soon as the shuttle was at 10,000 feet she would have to take over control and find a place to land. The shuttle passed from the blackness of space into the bright sunny atmosphere of the planet. When the shuttle reached the proper altitude the signal announced that the shuttle was ready for Mary to take control. She had practiced this many times on the simulator, but now her mind was blank.

"Oh, my gosh," she exclaimed, "I can't remember what to do."

But Mary hadn't trained for months in vain. As soon as she put her hands on the controls she began to automatically control the ship.

"Wow, I'm flying!" she shouted. "This is more fun than the simulator."

The controls felt natural in her hands and the shuttle maneuvered easily. The simulator's instructions ran through her mind: check display for altitude, fuel and attitude. Initiate visual search for a landing site.

She looked down at the planet. There was a carpet of dark green forest as far ahead as the eye could see. This was not good. She would have to find a clearing large enough to land the shuttle. She adjusted the shuttle to fly in a circle, surveying the horizon in all directions for a break in the trees. There appeared to be a change in the color of the ground cover at 184°. Mary pulled out of her turn and flew toward it. When she got close enough she could see that the forest had ended and there was a huge body of water. The forest extended almost to the edge of the water, but a narrow stretch of beach separated the forest from the water. Mary hoped she could use the beach to land, if she could find a stretch long enough.

As she descended she spotted what looked like a likely area and began her approach. She flew over the ocean parallel to the beach. She pressed the lever that lowered the wheels, then turned 90° and as the shuttle descended further she turned to her final approach. Mary kept the shuttle in a steady descent until it was just above the beach and then pulled up the nose so that the wheels barely touched the sandy beach as the forward motion of the shuttle slowed.

When the wheels finally settled into the sand the shuttle abruptly stopped, tipping the nose of the shuttle into the sand. Mary was jolted by the sudden stop and sat suspended by the safety belt for a few seconds. She moved her limbs cautiously and was relieved to find she was unhurt.

As she sat there, hanging from the safety belts, she exclaimed, "I did it! I really did it. All by myself I landed the shuttle!" Her hands still gripped the controls and sweat dripped from her face. She had never felt such elation. "If those snotty kids at school could see me now, I bet they would be jealous."

Finally she released her grip on the controls and unhooked the safety belt. She fell forward and bumped into the control panel. "Oops, I forgot about gravity," she giggled, still giddy and flushed with excitement.

She crawled to the airlock and managed to open the shuttle door. Somewhat awkwardly she climbed from the shuttle. Her legs felt weak as she stood on the beach. It had been a long time since she had felt the pull of gravity. She made her way around the shuttle to inspect the damage.

The shuttle was tipped forward on its nose and the wheels were buried in the sand. Otherwise it seemed intact. She was trying to figure out how she was going to get the shuttle out of the sand when she remembered she needed to contact X'akara. She quickly climbed back inside and pressed the communication button.

"X'akara, this is Mary," she said and waited for a reply.

"Mary, this is X'akara."

"X'akara, I have landed on a beach. The shuttle is stuck in sand, but appears intact. I do not know how I will get it out when it is time to return," Mary answered.

"Mary, remain near the shuttle. Do not waste fuel attempting to move it at this time. Take the hand-held communication device with you if you go outside. I will update my progress in three days."

Mary climbed back out of the shuttle, careful to take the hand-held communication device with her. She sat down in the sand and stared out over the water. Waves lapped at the shore and a warm breeze gently caressed her face. She was beginning to calm down and realized that she was quite tired. *I'll just close my eyes and rest for a few minutes,* she thought as she drifted off to sleep.

Mary awoke slowly and she stretched leisurely. For a moment she thought she was back at home in bed, but then she realized she was lying on sand. She sat up and looked around. She had slept much longer than she had intended and now it was night with only the pale light of the triple moons high above her illuminating the beach.

She got up and moved quickly to the shuttle. "I know it is silly to be scared of the dark, but I can't help it," she said as she climbed into the shuttle and closed the door. "I wish X'akara was with me," she cried as she slipped down to the floor and wrapped her arms around her legs feeling very sorry for herself. Her stomach growled and she knew she should eat something, but she was immobilized by sadness.

She didn't know how long she sat there lost in misery when she heard a noise outside the shuttle. She had just about convinced herself that she had imagined the sound when she felt the front of the shuttle being pulled from the sand. She crawled to the front of the ship and looked out. In front of the shuttle was an odd looking vehicle with huge wheels. It was a mottled dark green in color and the front part was open. Several large ropes stretched from somewhere under the ship and were attached to the vehicle. At the front sat a hooded figure that was frantically pulling a lever back and forth. Suddenly a puff of smoke spewed from the back of the vehicle and it began moving, tightening the ropes and dragging the shuttle behind it. Mary could see other hooded figures running along side the strange vehicle as it moved slowly toward the forest.

Mary stared with disbelief as the shuttle moved from the beach. She didn't know what to do and didn't move fast enough when one of the hooded figures spotted her. It raised its arm and a brilliant flash of light blinded her as she crumbled to the floor of the shuttle.

Chapter 7

Mary awoke with a start to find an elderly woman bending over her and looking intently into her eyes.

"Ah, young lady, I see you are finally awake," the woman said as Mary attempted to get up. "Please lie down a little longer. You have been stunned and it takes a while to recover. I am sorry you were hurt. Sometimes our young men over-react."

"Where am I?" Mary asked. "How did I get here?" She was confused and disoriented, but strangely she felt no fear.

"You are in my home. My grandson brought you here after you were stunned. The boys were upset that they had injured a child," the woman answered.

"Who are you? What are you doing here?" Mary asked. "I thought this planet was uninhabited."

"My name is Esmera, but everybody calls me Granny Mer and as you can see this planet is indeed inhabited, but we prefer that the rest of the universe think that it is uninhabited.

Suddenly Mary sat up, her head aching from the motion, "Where is my shuttle? I have to get back to my shuttle!"

"Now, now, child, if you mean your space ship please don't worry about it," said Granny Mer as she gently helped Mary to lie back down. "Your ship is safely hidden. We couldn't leave it out in the open on the beach. It is not safe. The bad ones could spot it there. Now you just rest while I prepare some food for you."

Mary looked around the small room. She was lying on a bed in one corner of the room under a shiny multicolored coverlet. Next to the bed was a padded bench and in the center of the room there was a table with 2 chairs. The fireplace was constructed of a prism-like transparent material through which the light from the flames was reflected in a multitude of colors. Hanging from the walls were dried plants tied with colored ribbons and strings.

Mary's stomach growled as Granny Mer lifted the lid from a pot hanging over the fire. A delicious smell filled the room as she ladled the soup into a bowl.

"I will let this cool a little while I help you sit up."

Granny Mer propped up Mary with pillows and placed a tray on her lap. She went to a cabinet beside the fireplace and brought out what appeared to be a large loaf of bread. She cut a thick slice and placed it in the soup. She smiled as she placed the food on the tray.

"Now, be careful Mary, that is still hot."

Mary dropped the utensil she had just picked up, "How did you know my name is Mary? I didn't tell you."

"Well, Mary, I read your thoughts." Granny Mer replied as if reading someone's mind was as normal as reading a book. "It is quite easy between Thayers. You are very easy to understand. Some folks are not."

Mary was perplexed by this information. "I don't understand. What's a Thayer?"

"You are a Thayer, my child, a person who can project their thoughts and receive another's thoughts. It should be very simple. But it is not so easy when you have a headache and are very hungry. Perhaps we will see what you can do later when you have had your fill and a little rest." Granny Mer said as she sat down next to Mary's Bed.

Mary gingerly tested the soup and found it was cool enough to eat. It was just as delicious as the aroma foretold.

"This is most delicious food I had ever eaten," she said as she lifted another bite of food to her mouth.

She secretly studied the face of her benefactor while she ate. Granny Mer was a small woman with silver hair pulled back tightly from her face and tucked into a black hat. The multitude of wrinkles made Mary think she must be very, very old. The most striking feature about Granny Mer was her eyes. Mary had never seen eyes with quite that shade of blue.

They seemed like deep pools of water and she felt herself being drawn into them.

She shook her head and turned her attention to the soup. She wasn't sure she believed what Granny Mer had told her about Thayers but she wasn't afraid. Something about Granny Mer made her feel safe and sheltered. That was a feeling Mary had never experienced except in dreams of her mother.

Granny Mer was overwhelmed with the thoughts and emotions that she received in that brief moment when Mary looked into her eyes. *What a bright little star you are,* she thought to herself. Never had she felt such raw unshielded power in a child. She sensed that Mary felt safe, but an underlying loneliness and melancholy was present. This beautiful creature had never been given the one thing every child craves. Granny felt a tear threaten to fall as she realized, *She has never felt a mother's love.* Her heart went out to this tiny child whose aura exhibited the very essence of bravery and honor.

When Mary finished the soup, Granny took the tray and settled Mary down in the bed.

"Rest now child. You will feel much better tomorrow," she said as tucked her into bed. She placed her hand on Mary's forehead and gently brushed back her hair, "You don't have a fever. That is good. Go to sleep now. I will be near if you need me."

Chapter 8

Somewhere in the bowels of the Bahadin Warship Falconoid a maintenance technician worked to repair the CAMCIA damaged in the unsuccessful attempt to capture Mary. Amden had been working on the robots for the entire voyage and hoped to stretch the job out as long as possible. Maintenance technicians typically had to do a lot of undesirable duties on the ship, such as unclogging sewer drains and repairing garbage grinders. This job was definitely cleaner and a lot easier. All he had to do to stay in the repair shop was to appear to be busy and do enough to satisfy his superior but not enough to complete all the repairs. It was a delicate balancing act. He certainly did not want to work on the sewers again. He had to crawl through the main sewer drain more than once and he didn't want to do that again.

Amden considered himself to be fairly intelligent and could work very hard if he enjoyed what he was doing. He didn't exactly like being a maintenance tech even though it was much better than being an ordinary slave. After he was sent to work on CAMCIA's he almost enjoyed his work. At times he all but forget how he came to be working on a Bahadin warship.

When he was a child he lived in a picturesque region of a lovely world called Lasovi. His father was a merchant and his mother was a well-known artist. He had two younger sisters, Jema and Dalee. Amden was studying to be an engineer and was doing well in school. He was a popular student and the girls at school thought he was very handsome with his curly blond hair and deep blue eyes. He wasn't vain enough to believe he was that good looking but he enjoyed the girls' attention.

That was before his planet was conquered and destroyed. He managed to survive the attack but was captured by the Bahadin. He was taken aboard a slave ship and thrown in the hold with all the other survivors. Days went by as Amden searched for his family and he had almost given up hope that they survived when he found his father and mother huddled in the dark, filthy hold. Sadly they never found his sisters.

Amden was taken to serve on first one and then another Bahadin warship. He started out the lowest of slaves, and after years of struggle he worked his way up to maintenance tech. He kept his anger in check and managed to keep his mouth shut, but he never forgot what the Bahadin had done to his home planet and his family. He vowed that some day he would have his revenge.

He shook his head. *I guess there is no use dwelling on the past,* he thought to himself. *I better stop daydreaming and get back to work.*

He turned his attention to the CAMCIA before him. He was a little puzzled by this one. It seemed a little different from the rest. It looked more like a servant class CAMCIA than a soldier CAMCIA. He couldn't tell for sure because the front breastplate was severely damaged. Both arms were missing as well. "Must have taken a direct hit from the looks of it," he said. He replaced the arms with new parts and used a breastplate from a CAMCIA that had a malfunctioning central processing unit.

"Well, old boy, if you were a servant before, you're a soldier now," he said to the CAMCIA.

He didn't expect an answer; the CAMCIA had been powered down during the repairs. He always powered down CAMCIA's when he worked on them because he didn't want to hear their constant jabbering. "Blasted things think they are smarter than me," he often told the fellows in the slave quarters.

The CAMCIA was secured in a harness that was suspended from a track on the ceiling. He pushed the CAMCIA back against the wall and secured it with heavy metal restraints. It was necessary to do this when powering up a damaged unit. Sometimes the central processing unit was flawed and a defective CAMCIA could do a lot of damage if it wasn't restrained. He checked to be sure the restraints were securely fastened and then opened the access panel and pressed the switch that would activate the CAMCIA. He was careful to jump out of the way as the CAMCIA's CPU powered up. The CAMCIA straightened up and each limb was flexed as the

CPU ran its diagnostic checks. Within a few minutes the CAMCIA opened its eyes and focused on the maintenance Tech.

X'orige did not recognize the man in front of him, but concluded from his uniform that he was a Bahadin maintenance tech.

So far, so good, thought the tech. "CAMCIA, run a complete system check, auto correct and report." He said as he picked up his clipboard computer to record the response.

"Systems check complete, one error found in section 5-Q7, corrected. One upper extremity control sequence non-standard configuration detected, corrected. Power system controls access panel door open. Unable to close because of upper extremity restraints," X'orige answered. He scanned the surrounding compartment while the tech recorded his response. He was positive now that he had succeeded in being taken aboard the Bahadin ship.

The tech, satisfied that the CAMCIA was not going to malfunction, finished writing his report, reached over to shut the access panel door and released the restraints.

He then consulted his clipboard computer again. "Report ID number and classification."

X'orige hesitated only a split second before responding, "Unable to report ID number or classification. Information lost or missing."

X'orige knew his ID number would not be in the records of the ship and he didn't want them to know that he wasn't one of their CAMCIA so he lied. He also knew that the Bahadin believed all CAMCIA's were unable to lie when questioned directly and to some extent this was true, but X'orige was no ordinary CAMCIA. His programmer had installed an experimental chip that allowed X'orige to evaluate a situation and fabricate information as needed.

"Hum, never had that happen before," Amden said. He went over to the desk and consulted the main repair console.

"CAMCIA unable to report ID or calcification," he spoke into the microphone.

A stream of information flashed across the screen, much too quickly for the tech to read except for the last line.

"Well, according to this, I can either tear your logic boards apart and try to find the bad sector, or if you are functioning properly otherwise, just assign you another ID number and classification."

Amden wasn't enthusiastic about completing all the requests and forms that he would have to go through to request a new ID number and classification. Some Bahadin officer would likely make an inquiry into why this particular CAMCIA didn't know his ID or classification. That would likely bring other officers down to check on the problem. Amden didn't want to have to deal with a bunch of officers looking for trouble. On this ship you definitely didn't want to draw attention to yourself.

He thought about it for a few minutes and looked around the repair area for a likely candidate to donate an ID number. "Let's see," he said as he checked the clipboard computer, "This CAMCIA has a defective CPU. I'll just assign his ID and classification to you. CAMCIA, your ID is 0301-08, and your classification is soldier grade II. Understood?"

"ID 0301-8, classification soldier grade II. Understood."

Amden removed the CPU from the former CAMCIA 0301-8, plugged a line from the external port to the diagnostic computer, and gave it instructions to format the CAMCIA's hard drive. *That will wipe out any evidence that I stole that CAMCIA's ID. Can't be too careful,* he thought as the computer completed the format.

He was straightening up the repair compartment when the door slid open and his superior walked in.

Amden bowed his head and lowered his eyes in the submissive posture that was expected of all slaves. He was well aware that to look directly at the Bahadin Officer would have been cause for severe punishment.

"How are the repairs coming?" the officer snarled.

"This CAMCIA needs to be reprogrammed. The CPU must have got a direct hit and erased most of the hard drive." Amden answered as the officer walked around the compartment. "I was formatting the few sectors that were left. I just finished with this one, a soldier grade II. It had a lot of damage. I had to replace both arms, but the CPU is in good shape. Powered up just fine."

"How soon can you have one programmed to serve as attendant to the Commander? He decided he didn't like the last one. What is left of it is outside on a cart. You probably won't be able to salvage many parts. He wants a new one as soon as possible," the officer said with a shake of his head.

Amden was very familiar with the Commander's penchant for destroying CAMCIA. This was not the first time he had to find a replacement for the Commander.

"I'll get right on that sir. Have one for you today," he answered as he wondered where he would find one capable of withstanding the violence that Commander's dark mood swings brought about. Rumor had it that CAMCIA's weren't the only ones destroyed by the Commander. He didn't want to find out first hand.

After the officer left the compartment Amden brought the cart with what was left of the Commander's CAMCIA into the compartment. He shook his head as he inspected the damage.

"Well I guess I will have to program another CAMCIA for the Commander. This one sure can't be fixed," he said as he started searching his records for a likely candidate to serve the Commander. Then he remembered the newly repaired CAMCIA.

"CAMCIA 0301-8 your structure looks a lot like a servant class. Were you ever programmed for personal service before you were a soldier?" he asked.

It would be lucky for him if the CAMCIA was already programmed. It would save him a lot of time.

"I was programmed as a servant class CAMCIA originally. I was captured and reassigned." X'orige answered.

"Did you retain your servant programming?"

"Affirmative."

"Well CAMCIA 0301-8 this is your lucky day. You have just been reassigned as a servant class. Just let me find the proper uniform and I will have you presented to the Commander."

Chapter 9

Mary was dreaming about her mother when she slowly awakened. She felt the warm glow and sense of security that the dream always gave her and she didn't want to loose that feeling. She stretched in the luxury of the soft bed feeling the weight of the warm bedding and the smell of fresh linen.

Ah, this is almost as good as the dream, she thought as her eyes opened to see Granny Mer sitting on the bench by the bed.

Granny Mer watched as Mary slowly awakened and when she opened her eyes said, "Contenza Mary. How are you feeling today?"

Mary smiled at Granny Mer and said, "I think I feel much better. Thank you for taking such good care of me."

"Oh, child, it was my pleasure to care for you. You are a very good patient."

Mary lifted the coverlet and started to get out of bed. She felt a little strange having all this loving attention bestowed on her by Granny Mer.

"No, No don't try to get up just now, Mary," Granny exclaimed. "Sit up for a while before you try to get up. Your body had a pretty bad shock last night."

Mary found that she was a little dizzy and decided to follow Granny's advice. But then she remembered X'akara and attempted to get up again, "But I have to wait in the shuttle for X'akara to call me."

"Who is X'akara, Mary?" Granny asked.

Mary paused for a moment. She knew that X'akara had warned that she should be careful what she told a stranger, but she felt so safe and comfortable with Granny Mer that she answered, "She is a CAMCIA. I lived with her and X'orige on Earth. I thought they were my parents until the night the Bahadin attacked our home and we had to leave. X'akara and I escaped in our ship but X'orige stayed behind. I don't know what happened to him," Mary answered, feeling sad remembering that frightening night. "X'akara is repairing our ship so we can go back to Ayri. She told me that I was born there but I don't remember it."

"Why did you leave your ship?"

"Something happened to it while were in hypervelocity. X'akara had to take us out of hypervelocity so she could fix the damage. The oxygen generator was damaged too so she said I would have to leave the ship and wait on this planet until it was safe for me to come back."

"Mary, who flew the shuttle here. Is there another CAMCIA with you?" Granny asked.

There was only X'akara and me on the ship. I had been practicing on the computer simulator while we were traveling. X'akara told me she didn't have time to bring me and that I could do it, and you know what? I did!" Mary exclaimed feeling very proud.

Granny shook her head in disbelief, not that Mary could fly the shuttle, she was well aware of Mary's intelligence, but that the CAMCIA had allowed a small child to pilot a shuttle to a supposedly uninhabited planet alone. *How,* she wondered, d*id that machine think Mary could survive alone?*

Mary continued, unaware of Granny's indignation. "So you see, I have to wait in the shuttle so when X'akara calls I can go back."

"Now, don't you worry about that child. Arman is looking after your shuttle. He'll let you know when your CAMCIA calls."

It was Mary's turn to be confused. "Who is Arman?" she asked.

"He's my grandson; the one that brought you here last night. He feels very bad about you getting hurt, so he'll take care of your shuttle. Now let me fix you some breakfast so you can get your strength back," Granny said as she shuffled across the room to the kitchen area.

Mary looked around at her surroundings. The room appeared smaller this morning with bright sunlight streaming in the windows. The light looked funny to Mary and she thought something was not quite right. With a shrug she decided not to worry about it right now.

Soon the smell of something delicious was coming from Granny's kitchen area and Mary's stomach growled. Granny brought a heaping plate on a tray to Mary as she sat in the bed.

"I think I can get up now," Mary said.

"I think you better stay in the bed a little longer, Mary. At least until you have broken your night fast.

When Mary began eating, the food was as delicious as the previous meal, but different.

"What is this stuff? It sure is good," Mary asked between bites.

"Syra eggs and bashut hash." Granny answered with a smile. "I'm glad you like it. It's my favorite morning food."

Mary was just finishing her meal when the door opened and a young man entered the cabin. The first thing that Mary noticed about him was that he was very tall and had to stoop to get through the door. His long black hair was tied back with a colorful filament.

"Contenza Granny," he said as he leaned over and gave her a kiss on cheek. "Something smells good! Have you got any leftovers for your favorite grandson? I'm about to starve."

Granny Mer smiled and said, "About to starve are you, Arman? When have you ever come in here not about to starve? Mary, can't you see how my poor grandson is wasting away from lack of food?" Her affection for this towering young man showed plainly on her face.

The smile on the young man's face faded as he noticed Mary lying in bed. He walked over and kneeled down beside her.

He took her hand and said, "I'm so sorry you were hurt last night. I know it's not a good excuse but the guys were very nervous about moving a strange ship. They didn't recognize the design and they were afraid it might be a new type Bahadin spy ship. When Nolus saw a movement in the ship he fired before he thought."

Mary stared open mouthed at the man who held her hand. She thought he was the most handsome man she had ever seen. She felt giddy and tongue-tied but finally managed to say, "I'm feeling better," and felt herself blushing.

Arman patted her hand and gave her a smile that set her heart fluttering. "Well, I'm glad to hear you are feeling better," he said as he turned his attention to the food his grandmother put on the table. "Is that for me?"

Granny watched Mary's reaction to Arman and felt the tingle of emotion that radiated from her. *Ah, there's another heart he has stolen with that smile,* she thought. *And he doesn't even know.* A lot of young women had set their hearts on Arman but he had eyes for only one. He had loved Sachel since they were children and soon they would marry. Granny knew that many hearts were broken when their contract was announced.

"Granny, what's got you daydreaming?" Arman asked between bites.

"Oh, nothing much, Arman. Just thinking about how it seems that only yesterday you were a tiny baby and now you are all grown up and getting ready for your wedding," Granny answered with a sigh.

Arman paused and looked at his grandmother with a twinkle in his eyes. "Oh Granny, I'm sorry I grew up and broke your heart. You know I will always love you the most," Arman said as he reached for Granny's hand.

"Oh, go on with you, Arman," Granny said as she playfully swatted his outstretched hand. "You just love my cooking."

Mary was listening to the conversation with interest and found she was feeling a little jealous. *Oh, I would just die if he said he loved me!* she thought as she suppressed a giggle.

Granny watched her grandson with a smile as he consumed the food she placed on the table for him. While he was eating Granny told Arman how Mary came to be in the space shuttle sitting on the beach. She ended by saying, "So you can call off the search for the pilot of the shuttle. Mary was the pilot."

"What!" he exclaimed, "Mary flew the ship?" He turned to look at Mary with disbelief. "You can fly a shuttle, Mary?"

Mary felt her face flush bright red but in spite of her sudden shyness she was able to answer, "Yes I can."

Arman looked at her with a new respect. He was beginning to realize that she was no ordinary child.

When Arman finished eating and was starting to leave he paused and turned to speak to Mary again. "I have been keeping your communicator with me. The Council didn't want you to contact your ship until they were sure that you weren't a threat even though Granny told them last night that she would vouch for you. They trust Granny, but they still want to ask you some questions. I will continue to keep the communicator with me and monitor it for you in the meantime. You take care and get better soon. I'm very sorry you were hurt."

"Thank you, Arman." Mary said and watched as he bent down to exit the room.

"Granny, he is the most handsome man I have ever seen!" Mary said with a sigh.

"Thank you, I think so too, but I am prejudiced since he is my grandson." Granny answered with a smile.

Mary suddenly remembered that Granny was a Thayer. "Granny, is he a Thayer too? Could he read my thoughts? I would just die if he knew what I was thinking!"

Granny paused, and thought for a moment, "Yes, he is a Thayer, but he shields. Not everyone here is a Thayer and it would be inappropriate for him to listen to others thoughts. He will only hear what you want him to hear. I taught him to respect the privacy of others when he was a small child."

Later that morning Granny helped Mary to get up. "Would you like to take a bath, Mary? I think it would make you feel better."

"Oh, I would love a bath," Mary answered. "I haven't had a real bath in a long time. You can't take a real bath on a space ship."

"I know," Granny answered. "Have you had a long journey?"

"It's been about 1 year space normal time. I think that's what X'akara told me the last time I asked."

Granny pushed a button on the wall nearest the bed and the cabinet slid open to reveal a roomy bathing area with a huge sunken tub. She touched a switch on the wall and tiny lights illuminated the sides and bottom of the tub and warm water mixed with a fluorescent blue liquid flowed from two openings in the bottom of the tub. Immediately the room was filled with a wonderful fragrance and the lovely blue bubbles foaming in the tub intrigued Mary.

Mary was still a little weak, so Granny helped her undress and slip into the tub. She sighed as she relaxed in the warm water. "Ah, this is wonderful. It feels so good to soak in a tub of water. I never had bubbles before."

Mary splashed and played in the tub until her fingers and toes were wrinkled and the water became cold. Granny wrapped her in a large warm towel and helped dry her hair.

"Oh my gosh, I just remembered, I don't have any clean clothes!" Mary exclaimed.

"Now, now child. Don't you worry, I thought you might like to take a bath this morning so I borrowed some clothes from one of my granddaughters while you were sleeping. I think she is about your size."

The clothing Granny had for Mary was similar to the outfit that Granny was wearing. Even though Mary insisted that she was feeling better after her soak in the tub, Granny helped her get dressed.

First she guided Mary in putting on a garment that reminded Mary of a long sleeved white tee shirt, except it was incredibly soft and silky. Next she slipped on a pair of trousers made of the same soft material. Over this went a long dark green sleeveless tunic that reached just above her ankles. Gold embroidery decorated the neckline. A pair of dark green sandals completed the outfit. Mary felt wonderfully elegant in the flowing silky costume. She swirled around in front of the mirror admiring the beautiful fabric and the way it flowed around her. It was the most beautiful thing she had ever worn.

Granny's eyes grew a bit misty as she watched Mary turn to see herself in every angle. The child had obviously never had an opportunity to wear lovely things. Mary's uninhibited joy in wearing the beautiful clothing touched Granny's heart and she wanted to shelter this child, give her all the love and attention she had never experienced. But somehow Granny knew that Mary would have to leave soon and face her future alone. She hoped Mary would be strong enough to face her destiny; a destiny that Granny could feel was clouded with many dangers.

I can't protect her much longer, but I will try to make the time we have as enjoyable as possible, Granny thought.

Granny insisted that Mary rest for the remainder of the day and to keep her from being bored taught her how to play Copo, a simple game with few rules that was deceptively easy to learn but difficult to master.

Mary watched, as Granny placed small round pebbles on a numbered grid. She shuffled a stack of numbered cards and placed them face down on the table.

"Now Mary, take a card from the top of the stack. You have to remove the number of pebbles indicated on the card. The card also tells you if you have to remove all the pebbles from one row or from anywhere on the grid. You can remove more than the number on the card but not less. If you are unable to remove the correct number you will get one point for each pebble less than the specified number. If you remove the last pebble you will gain 100 points. The lowest number of points wins the game."

"That seems simple enough," Mary said but she soon found out that it required a lot of strategy, planning and luck to win.

They played until the light began to fade outside the windows and Granny announced it was time for Mary to go to bed.

Mary carefully folded her new clothes and placed them on the bench beside her bed.

"Here Mary, I have a sleeping dress for you to use," Granny said as she handed it to Mary.

"Oh," Mary said as she pulled the sleeping dress over her head, "This is a nightgown."

"I guess you could call it that," Granny said.

Granny sat on the bench next to the bed as Mary snuggled down in the warm covers.

"Granny, where are you going to sleep? Did I take your bed?" Mary sleepily asked.

"No Mary, you didn't take my bed. It is in the next room. Do you see the door beside the fireplace?"

Granny pulled the cabinet next to the fireplace out and Mary could see another room containing a bed.

"Do you hide everything behind cabinets?" Mary giggled.

"I guess we do. I never thought about it before." Granny answered with a smile. "Now go to sleep and I'll see you in the morning."

The next morning Granny gave Mary another beautiful outfit to wear. This one had a dark blue tunic over a pale yellow blouse and trousers. She watched with satisfaction as Mary delighted in her reflection in the mirror.

"Would you like to go with me to the market? That is if you are finished admiring yourself in the looking glass and feel up to it," Granny said as Mary made her fourth turn in front of the mirror.

"Yes, that would be great, Granny," Mary answered cheerfully.

Chapter 10

Granny picked up her basket and opened the door. When Mary stepped out of the door she stopped in amazement. She was totally unprepared for the scene before her. She expected to see a forest and perhaps a road or path winding through it. What she saw was a well-lighted tunnel about 10 feet wide. On the wall opposite Granny's door was a painted mural of a forest scene.

"Wow, Granny, what's this?" a puzzled Mary asked.

"Wasn't what you expected was it, Mary?" Granny replied with a chuckle. "My home as well as all the other homes on this planet are underground. My children had them to make my living space to resemble my first home on Quain because I missed it so much. It really was a lovely place surrounded by a beautiful forest. I missed it so much"

"You mean everybody lives underground?" Mary asked. "Why?"

"Come, let us walk toward the Central Cavern and I will try to explain," Granny said as they made their way along the tunnel. "A long time ago on another planet called Quain we lived on the surface. It was a lovely place, a lot like the planet above us. Then the bad ones attacked our planet."

"Bad Ones?" Mary asked, "Could they be the Bahadin that attacked my home?"

"Yes, Mary, I believe they are probably the same. Anyway they systematically destroyed everything and everyone they encountered. The leaders in the Capital City tried to negotiate with them or find some way to understand why they had attacked. There was no reasoning with them. They gathered all the citizens of the capital in the plaza and brutally executed our leaders in front on them. Then they started loading everyone onto slave ships. Anyone who offered resistance was killed."

"How did you manage to escape?"

Granny paused a moment as the memory of the terror and fear threatened to overwhelm her and then continued, "We lived far away from the Capital in a rural area. We received reports that the Capital had fallen and we knew we would be next. We had no weapons to fight the Bad Ones but we did have space ships that we had used for transporting our grain and food to other planets. We loaded our families and supplies on the ships and left our home behind. It was cramped and uncomfortable in the supply ships. They were never intended to transport people but somehow we managed. We traveled far from our home in search of a place similar to our planet. It took many long years of space travel before we found this planet. We called it New Quain. But even here we didn't feel safe. Everyone was afraid that the Bad Ones would come and destroy this home as well. That's when the Council came up with a plan to fool the Bad Ones. It was well known that they never bother to attack an uninhabited planet so we decided to hide our homes by building everything underground."

"But how did you dig all these tunnels? It must have taken a long time."

"Our ships were equipped with laser cannons that were used to destroy asteroids that often were a problem in the shipping lanes in space. The cannons weren't strong enough to fight against the Bad ones but they worked wonderfully digging the tunnels. We were able to blast out a pleasant underground world in a very short time. We used almost everything on the ships to make our home comfortable. For example the trade ships had light sources that they used to grow plants for food. We mounted them in the central tunnel so we could grow our food down here. Now the planet above gives the appearance of being uninhabited while we are safe below."

"How did you know I had landed on the surface if you all stay underground all the time?" Mary asked.

"We have sensors hidden on the surface," Granny answered, "We need to keep a close watch on the surface. Who knows when the bad ones will do next?"

Mary walked along as she listened to Granny's story. She saw that even though the tunnel was far below the surface it was wide and well ventilated and was beautifully decorated.

"It is so beautiful, here. It makes me forget we are underground," Mary said.

"The tunnels were bare and ugly when we first moved into them. When my 'Forest Home' was almost complete we hired an artist to paint the mural on the wall in front. Some of the other families liked the idea and began painting their spaces. Now, almost every inch of the tunnels is decorated. It does help make it more cheerful."

"Do you ever wish you could live on the surface?" Mary asked.

"Yes, I do miss it, but most of our children don't remember living on the surface. They are more comfortable in the tunnels. I guess its all what you get used to."

"You know," Mary said, "I thought the light coming through your windows looked odd, but I couldn't quite figure out what was wrong with it."

"Yes, it isn't exactly like sunlight, but I have grown used to it. It's programmed to turn on and off to simulate day and night. I thought it was very clever."

They came to the end of the tunnel and walked through an arched doorway. Once again Mary was amazed and surprised by the scene in front of her. A huge cavern stretched high above her with the floor far below. All around the cavern at regular intervals from top to bottom were arched doorways opening onto walkways protected by ornate metal railings. Ramps spiraled down connecting the levels and 2 large glass enclosed elevators moved quietly up and down the wall on opposite sides of the cavern. The entire floor of the cavern was covered with a patchwork quilt of cultivated fields. A yellow glow emanated from the very top of the cavern, bathing the entire space with a sunny glow.

"Gosh, Granny, it almost feels like we walked outside," an astonished Mary exclaimed. "Look at the elevators! I bet they are fun to ride. Are we going to ride the elevator?" she asked hopefully.

"Well, Mary, the market is on this level, but if you would like we can ride the elevator to the bottom and have a look at the fresh produce." Granny replied with a twinkle in her eye. She had always liked to ride the elevator and now she had the added pleasure of watching Mary enjoying herself.

Granny and Mary joined the queue waiting on the elevator and within minutes they were on their way to the bottom of the cavern.

The elevator was made entirely of glass, including the floor. Mary felt a little dizzy and a tingle of excitement when she looked down. *This must be what it is like to be on a ride at an amusement park,* she thought as the elevator glided quietly and surprisingly rapidly toward the ground floor. Mary had often heard children back on Earth talking about trips to amusement parks and wondered what it would be like. *If it were anything like this*, she thought, *I would definitely like a thrill ride.*

As they neared the bottom of the cavern Mary could see the workers harvesting food and cultivating the fields. Near the elevator there were large shelves notched from the stone wall where the fruits and vegetables were proudly displayed. There was an abundance of produce in a multitude of colors, none of which were familiar to Mary.

They strolled among the stands and Granny pointed out varieties and explained, "Most of what you see is vegetable produce. The large red ones are setam, and the dark purple ones are eyegab. The oblong grayish white root is bashut. We dice it and cook it with the ground meat of the bopair. You had that this morning. I am particularly fond of the little green sepas, but they are hard to prepare. They are very poisonous if you don't remove all the skin and the inner core."

Even though Mary enjoyed watching Granny carefully examining the available products and hearing the exotic names, she was anxiously awaiting the return trip on the elevator.

When Granny had finished shopping they rode back to their level. The trip up the wall of the cavern was even more thrilling to Mary than the ride down, but all too soon they reached their destination and had to exit.

"Wow! That was fun Granny, thank you for taking me," Mary exclaimed, "I loved it!"

"Thank you, Mary. I have to admit I enjoy the ride as well. You know some people can't stand it and have to walk down the incline ramps."

It was just a short walk from the elevator to the market that was located in a large brightly lit tunnel. Shops were situated on both sides of the tunnel. Over the shops were cloth banners in a dazzling array of colors with the shop's names embroidered in large letters. Mary tilted her head back to read the names on the closest shops: "Paters Cooking Containers and Other Essentials", "Cottier's Handmade Garments", "Soo's Footgear", "Gosman's Preserved Edibles". Samples of the shop's wares were proudly displayed in metal bins out front and the proprietors politely urged the shoppers to come and see the wonderful things inside.

Granny went about her shopping with a curious Mary by her side. Soon she was finished and they walked back to her home. When they got there, Granny bustled about putting away her purchases humming as she worked.

Mary suddenly realized she was very tired and sat down at the table and rested her head on her arms. Granny turned around to find Mary sound asleep and gently picked her up and placed her on the bed. Mary was so very tired that she didn't awake even when Granny undressed her and tucked her in bed. Granny neatly folded Mary's clothes and placed them on the trunk at the foot of the bed, along with the new clothes that she had purchased for Mary that day. She hummed as she worked and was enjoying taking care of a young one.

"Ah, I didn't know how much I missed caring for a child," she said to herself, "I hope Arman provides me with lots of little great-grand children."

For now she was content caring for Mary, even though she knew that Mary would have to leave soon. Somewhere far away Mary's destiny awaited her on another planet.

Chapter 11

Mary awoke once again to the wonderful smell of Granny's cooking. She sat up, rubbing her eyes and said, "How long have I been asleep?"

"You slept all afternoon and through the night, Mary. I'm glad. You needed to rest. It takes a long time to recover from being stunned," Granny answered. "If you are ready to get up, you can freshen up in the bathing room. I laid out your new clothes in there for you."

Mary hopped out of bed and went into the bathing room. When she was finished dressing she came out to find Granny had placed the food on the table.

"Aren't you going to eat with me?" Mary asked as she sat down.

"I ate earlier this morning, but I think I may have just a little something just to be sociable."

"I'm glad to have your company. I always had to eat alone at home. I didn't know why until we had to leave and X'akara told me she was a CAMCIA. You know it's funny that I didn't wonder about that before now." Mary said as she began eating. "Gosh, I'm really hungry. I don't think I have ever tasted food this good!"

"Thank you, Mary," Granny said with a smile, "I enjoyed preparing it for you."

"What are we going to do today?" Mary asked.

"Would you like to go to the surface for a little while this morning?" Granny asked.

"Ooh, that would be great!" Mary exclaimed with excitement.

"Well, when you are through with your breakfast that's what we will do." Granny said with smile.

After they had finished eating Mary helped Granny clean the dishes and straighten the kitchen and then when they were ready to leave Mary started to go to the door.

"Not that way, Mary," Granny said, "I have a secret passage to the surface."

Mary followed Granny into the bathing room where Granny pulled back a curtain. Behind the curtain was a small closet with shelves for storage. When Granny pulled on one of the shelves the entire unit pulled out revealing a dark passage. She pressed a switch on the wall and the cave was illuminated with a faint light.

"When they finished the underground tunnels the engineers were supposed to seal all the passageways to the surface except the emergency escape tunnel. When they came to close this one I told them it was already closed. They were so busy they never bothered to check. Most folks were anxious to have the access tunnels into their homes closed. I guess I am the only person left who enjoys going to the surface." Granny said as they climbed the winding stairs inside the tunnel.

At the top of the stairs there was a landing and a metal cage. Above the cage the tunnel went straight up. They climbed inside the cage and it slowly began moving upward gaining momentum as it rose to the surface.

Mary couldn't see any ropes or mechanism attached to the cage and asked, "What makes this thing move, Granny?"

Granny was standing with her eyes closed and didn't answer until the cage had reached the top and the cage slid forward on to solid ground.

As they stepped out onto the forest floor Granny answered "I was making the cage move."

"But, how? You were just standing there with your eyes closed," Mary asked puzzled by Granny's answer.

"Closing my eyes helps me concentrate. I'm not as strong as I used to be. You will probably be able to do it with your eyes open with a little practice."

"Do what?" Mary asked, still not understanding what Granny's meaning.

"Telekinesis, moving objects with your mind," Granny said calmly as if she were talking about some mundane thing.

"Oh, sure, you might be able to do that, but not me, I'm just plain Mary. I don't have any special powers." Mary said as she looked at Granny in awe.

"But that is where you are very wrong, Mary. I have felt your power. You, my child, are very strong. You just need to learn how to harness that power."

"But I don't understand. How can I do that?" Mary asked still not believing she could possibly possess any special powers.

"Be patient and I'll show you how," Granny said as they walked to the center of the small clearing near the tunnel opening.

Mary looked around her and saw huge plants with twisted trunks reaching far up into the violet sky above the planet. The forest floor was as soft and spongy as a thick carpet. The air was filled with the fragrance of the wild flowers that grew in the few patches of sun that managed to penetrate the canopy of the tall plants. Mary could hear the sounds of soft bells tinkling.

"Where are the bells, Granny? I can't see them." Mary asked, looking for the source of the beautiful sounds.

"The sounds that you hear are the songbirds in the trees."

"Oh, how beautiful, they sound just like little bells."

"Now Mary, if you are ready we will begin your training," Granny said as she opened what appeared to be a large tree stump and pulled out a large round white ball.

Mary almost dropped the ball when Granny handed it to her. It was very heavy and appeared to be made of stone. Granny told Mary to hold the ball in front of her and to concentrate on making the ball lighter. The weight of the ball was causing Mary's arms to tremble but she gallantly gazed at the ball and willed it to become lighter. Nothing happened and soon Mary lost her grip on the ball and it fell to the forest floor.

"I told you I didn't have any powers," Mary said, just a little disappointed.

"You haven't given up yet, have you. You're just beginning. You have to learn how to use your powers just as you learned to walk. When you finally find the way to make the ball lighter you will be able to remember that feeling and each time it will become easier. Now pick up the ball and try again."

Mary did as she was told and concentrated on the ball. Her arms were straining under the weight of the ball when suddenly everything around her faded as she focused all her attention on the ball. It became lighter and then became weightless. Her arms stopped aching as the ball seemed to float in front of her and then slowly it began to rise. At this point Mary lost her grip on the ball and her concentration as well and the ball fell to the ground.

"Wow! Granny, I did it. I really did it. Did you see that!" Mary shouted as she danced around Granny. "Does this make me a witch or something?"

"Of course not. You are just an ordinary person who happens to have an extraordinary talent. Now practice making the ball lighter but hold it close to your chest. You should be able to lift yourself along with the ball," Granny instructed as she handed the ball to Mary.

Mary found that she could focus her attention on the ball without seeing it and she did rise with the ball a few feet in the air, but then she got excited and both she and the ball tumbled to the forest floor. With a little more practice she could rise with the ball, hover and then descend gently to the ground.

Granny sat on a stump and watched as Mary practiced. Then she beckoned to her and said, "That is enough for today. There is another more important trick that you must master. You must learn to shield your thoughts from other telepathic people. This is for your own privacy and their comfort. It is quite simple and could be very important."

Mary sat on the ground at Granny's feet and listened as she explained the technique.

"Close your eyes and picture a curtain coming down in front of your mind, a curtain so thick and impenetrable that no thought can escape. Keep concentrating until the curtain becomes as real as the forest around you," Granny explained.

Mary did as instructed and just as Granny said she could see and feel the curtain closing in her thoughts.

Granny felt suddenly alone and disconnected when Mary drew the curtain down. She missed the steady stream of innocent thoughts from the child. She was proud of the way Mary was able to learn the technique and she said, "Good job, Mary. When you need to communicate with someone, just imagine your thought slipping through the curtain to travel to the person you want to communicate with. No one else can hear your thoughts. Try to send a thought to me now."

Mary concentrated hard and pictured the words slipping through to Granny.

I LOVE YOU!

Granny was rocked by the force of the thought and had to grasp the side of the stump to steady herself. "I love you too, Mary, but next time don't put so much force behind the thought. You nearly knocked me off the stump," Granny said with a chuckle, as she rubbed her forehead. "Why don't you go and levitate until I recover."

Mary walked back into the clearing and was searching for the ball when Granny said, "You don't need the ball anymore. Just think of becoming lighter and lighter, but don't get too high. You might get hurt if you lose your concentration."

Soon Mary was able to soar above the ground and move across the clearing with ease. She felt so free. She looked down to where Granny was sitting and was just about to call out to her when she saw Arman enter the clearing. She completely lost her concentration and crashed down in front of him. She felt herself turning red as she spun away from him to brush the twigs and leaves from her face.

Oh! She thought to herself, *Why am I such a mess every time he is around?*

She could hear Arman talking to Granny and he didn't sound happy.

"Contenza, Granny. Did you know that you left the door to the passageway open again? You know that if anyone came in and find it and you would be in a lot of trouble. No one is supposed to go to the surface without official permission," he said, shaking his head.

Granny just smiled at him and said, "I'm sorry I worried you. It was foolish of me to leave the door open."

Arman couldn't help but smile back at his grandmother. She was a wonderful person, even if she was careless with the door to the passage to the surface. He loved her dearly and remembered clearly the times she had taken him to this very place to learn to control his powers and to respect the privacy of others.

Granny always told him, "Never invade the thoughts of another without their knowledge, especially if that person is a non-Thayer. The power of a Thayer is awesome and not to be taken lightly."

Arman always tried to obey his grandmother and did his best to live up to her standards. Besides, she always knew when he misbehaved. She was so proud the day he was able to transport himself up the passage without the cage.

He turned his attention to Mary then, "Mary are you injured? I saw you take a tumble."

"It's her first lesson, Arman," Granny said, "I think she is doing remarkably well."

Arman looked at Granny in surprise and then turned back to Mary. "Your first lesson? That's impressive, Mary. You are doing a lot better than I did. I couldn't even levitate the ball on my first lesson. The most important thing you have to remember is to keep your concentration when you fly. I took many a tumble before I learned that!"

Mary was unable to say much more than "I'm all right," because of her extreme embarrassment and to add to her discomfort, Arman took her arm to help her up and brushed the twigs and leaves from her hair and dress.

"I'm glad you are alright," he said as he brushed the last piece of moss from Mary's hair. "I almost forgot why was looking for you. Your CAMCIA has been calling on your communicator. I know the council won't like it if I let you contact your ship but Granny and I think you should answer."

He handed the communicator to Mary and she pressed the call button and said "X'akara, this is Mary."

A few seconds later the communicator cracked to life and they heard, "Mary, this X'akara. I have been able to fire engines to halt degradation of the orbit. Additional repairs remain to be accomplished. Will contact with update in three days."

The communicator went silent and Mary handed it back to Arman and said "Thanks for letting me contact X'akara."

Arman put the communicator back in his pocket and shook his head, "She sure was a friendly CAMCIA."

It took Mary a few seconds to realize that he was joking. She smiled self-consciously and replied "Aren't all CAMCIA like that?"

"Well, we don't have many here, but the ones that I have seen have been programmed to have a little more personality than that one. You can do it if you can find the service book," Arman answered. "Now we all need to get back down the passage before someone else comes looking for you two."

Mary reluctantly joined Granny in the cage and they descended. Arman chose to descend on his own. Mary wanted to try it by herself, but didn't want to risk having another accident in front of Arman.

When they got back to Granny's home Arman closed the door to the tunnel and turned to his grandmother.

"Granny, please be careful. The council is watching you closely because Mary is staying with you. I know you don't want them to find the tunnel. They would surely have it sealed."

Granny breathed a heavy sigh. She knew Arman was only trying to protect her.

Arman gave his grandmother a hug and said, "Got to go. Bosahalo Lipizn is competing in a Cringalingling match in the Level Eight Arena tonight and I don't want to miss that. Contenza Granny and Mary."

"Contenza Arman."

That night Mary was unusually quiet. The communication from X'akara reminded her that she had to leave New Quain. It was something she wished she didn't have to do.

Finally she told Granny she was tired and went to bed only to lie awake for most of the night.

Chapter 12

The next morning before Granny awoke Mary slipped quietly out of bed. She wrote a short note to Granny explaining that she needed a little time alone and left it on the table. Then she slipped into the bathing room and opened the door to the hidden tunnel to the surface. She was very careful to close the access door behind her. Then she scrambled up the stairs to the cage, climbed inside and sat on the floor. She closed her eyes and concentrated on making the cage lighter. Slowly the cage began to rise but Mary was afraid to open her eyes until she could feel the warm glow of sunlight fill the cage as it slid out onto the landing at the top. She knew then that it was safe to exit the cage and she stepped out into the clearing.

It felt good to be in the open space alone. Mary sat on a stump and thought about all the things that had happened to her. She was happier than she ever had been in her life, but the call from X'akara yesterday reminded her that she would have to go back to the ship as soon as the repairs were finished. She would miss the wonderful people here, especially Granny. It made her very sad to think about leaving the only friends she had ever made. Here, alone in this lovely place, she let her pent up emotions free. The tears flowed freely and her heart felt as if it were breaking.

"Why do I have to go," she sobbed. But even in the depths of her sorrow something deep inside reminded Mary that her destiny was not here.

Slowly Mary became aware of a warm, soft furry thing resting quietly beside her. She wiped away her tears and blinked her eyes to focus on a small ball of black and white fur that was gently vibrating as it snuggled close to her foot. She leaned over to touch the small animal and it arched its little head to meet her hand.

"Well, what to we have here?" Mary said softly as she picked up the animal and placed it in her lap.

When she picked it up it retracted its head and became round as a ball with no distinguishable head or legs, but as soon as it was safely in her lap, out popped its little head to look at Mary. Its tiny head was covered with black and white fur. Its face was dominated by its large round eyes, and a wide mouth that seemed to be smiling at Mary. As she looked into the smiling eyes of the little animal she felt a rush of love and tenderness.

"Oh, you sweet little thing," she cooed to the little fur ball. It snuggled down in her lap and arched its little head to meet Mary's hand as she rubbed its soft fur.

She lost all track of time as she sat contented in the warm sunshine rubbing the affectionate little animal. She was so engrossed in petting her little friend that she didn't know Granny had joined her until Granny spoke.

"Mary, what are you holding?"

Mary smiled at Granny and held up the tiny animal for Granny to see. "I don't know. I never saw anything quite like it before but it is the most adorable, affectionate little creature I have ever saw."

Why, it's a little barda," Granny said with a chuckle. "I didn't know there were any wild ones left on the surface. They're very affectionate and they make excellent companions."

Mary looked down at the ball of fluff in her lap. "He makes me happy. I was crying and he just showed up and snuggled to my side and I felt better. Can I keep him?"

"I think you must keep him. It sounds like you have already bonded with that little barda," Granny said with a smile. "It is a rare privilege to belong to a barda. You should feel honored to have been chosen. But right now, Mary, we need to get back down the shaft so you can have your breakfast before it gets cold."

Mary stood up cradling her new friend in her arms and walked to the cage. "What do I feed him Granny? I think he's hungry."

"It will eat what ever you eat. Such is the way of the barda. Do you want to try to go down the shaft without the cage this time Mary?"

"I don't know. I'm afraid I will drop my little barda. He is just a little baby," Mary answered with a look of concern on her face.

"Don't worry, he won't fall. If you drop him he will just fly along side you."

Mary looked down at the tiny barda and said, "You can fly? Does my little barda have wings?"

As if to answer her, he stretched his tiny wings launched himself from her hand and flew up to land on Mary's head. Mary couldn't help but giggle at the adorable little barda.

As they were floating down the tunnel Granny asked, "Do you know what its name is yet?"

Mary thought a minute and said, "You know I do know his name. It's Biz! His name just popped into my head. Is that the way it happens with everybody?"

"That's what everyone tells me," Granny answered, "I never had one, though I know a lot of people who do."

"Can I take him with me when I have to leave? Do you think he will want to go with me?" Mary asked anxiously, suddenly saddened at the thought of possibly leaving Biz behind, but willing to do whatever was best for him.

"You have to take him with you now. Once you have bonded with a barda you can never leave him. He would die if separated from you. They are very loyal little creatures and he will love and defend you with his life.

He would rather die than see you hurt and I'm sure you feel the same way. It only takes a few seconds to bond with a barda but that bond lasts for life."

Mary reached up and removed the little barda from her head and held him close to her heart. Biz snuggled closer and with a contented sigh closed his eyes and went to sleep.

Chapter 13

Over the next few days Mary practiced using her power to move objects and concentrated on shielding her thoughts. Granny could feel Mary's power growing even stronger and guided her in the proper use of that power.

During this time Mary was also learning the joy of belonging to a barda. Biz really wasn't much trouble and was quite playful. She also learned that her sweet little pet was anything but defenseless. His mouth while mostly curved into a sweet smile contained a set of very sharp teeth and his little feet had retractable claws that could do quite a bit of damage if he chose. But with Mary he was always gentle. Mary found it hard to imagine life without him.

During this time X'akara would contact Mary every three days with updates on the ship repairs. Each time Arman would bring the communicator to Mary and they would go to the surface to answer. Arman cautioned Mary to not mention anything about the people inhabiting the planet and never to let anyone on the planet know she was communicating with the ship. On the last communication X'akara indicated that the repairs were almost complete and Mary was to prepare to leave. Mary fought back her tears as she and Arman traveled down the tunnel to tell Granny the news.

When Mary saw Granny standing in the kitchen she broke into tears and ran to hug her. Granny knew this day was coming and felt her heart breaking as she held the sobbing child. Arman slipped quietly out the door and left them alone. He too had grown fond of Mary and would miss her as well.

"Now, now Mary. I know it makes you sad to think about leaving, and my heart is breaking too but we have a few more days together and we must make the most of them. Besides that you are upsetting Biz." Granny said as the fought to control her tears.

Biz was flitting around Mary and Granny, in a nervous state. He didn't know what was troubling Mary but he could feel she was upset. He finally landed on her head and began rubbing her hair with his chin. He radiated warmth and comfort and Mary felt his calming effect.

"Oh Biz, you are so special. How did I ever live without you?" Mary said wiping away her tears and gathering him into her arms.

Granny watched as Mary cuddled her tiny pet and was glad that at least Mary would have the comfort of Biz when it came time to return to the ship.

How, she wondered, *did that loving and kind child exist without someone or something to love her in return?*

A knock on the front door interrupted Granny's thoughts. She went to the door and spoke with someone and then came back to where Mary stood. It was obvious that Granny was upset.

"What's wrong Granny?" Mary asked.

"That was a messenger from the council," Granny said, "You are being summoned to appear at the Council Chamber tomorrow."

Granny's somber tone of voice sent a shiver of fear through Mary. "Did the messenger say what they want with me?" Mary asked in a trembling voice.

"The messenger didn't say, but I expect they want to ask you why you are here and what you intend to do. I was hoping that they wouldn't get around to your case until after you returned to your ship."

"What will they do to me?"

"I think they will probably just want to ask you some questions."

"Will you go with me tomorrow?"

"I will go with you to the Council Chamber, but you will have to go inside alone. Just answer their questions honestly. Don't hold anything back. They will know if you are not sincere."

Granny patted Mary's hand and with enormous effort she shielded her fears from Mary. She was deeply afraid for her, but she didn't want Mary know. It would be easier for Mary if she faced the Council without fear clouding her brain. Granny knew the Council was fair but they might decide that Mary was too dangerous to have on the planet. They had to consider the welfare of all the people.

Despite Granny's efforts to shield, Mary felt Granny's fear. They tried to be cheerful but the effort was very taxing on both Mary and Granny. Biz flitted around nervously and barely ate the food that Mary offered him.

"I think Biz is sick," Mary said with a note of concern in her voice.

"He feels your anxiety, Mary. He will be fine when you settle down. Just cuddle him in your arms and you both will feel better."

All too soon it was time for bed and although she was very tired Mary was afraid she wouldn't be able to sleep at all but with Biz snuggled close she was able to sleep a little. She feared what the morning would bring and wished she could stop the clock, but morning came despite her wishes.

Chapter 14

Granny and Mary were just about ready to leave for the meeting when they heard a knock on the door. When Granny opened the door she was surprised to see Arman and Nolus.

Before Granny could speak Arman said, “We heard about the summons from the Council and we want to go with you.”

It was a quiet group that made their way through the tunnel and into the central tunnel. Mary had Biz cradled in her arms and his presence helped calm her. Instead going to the elevators they turned to the left and entered another tunnel. This tunnel led to a transport center where high-speed pods carried travelers to destinations deep within the interior of the planet. The Council Chamber was the last and deepest station.

Mary watched as Granny placed her hand over what appeared to be a light on a metal rail. With a beep a small metallic object was ejected from an opening in the rail and began blinking.

“What is that? Mary asked.

“It’s a control module,” Granny said, “I have to enter our destination and the number of passengers.”

Granny pressed a lighted button and once again the object beeped. She then pressed the button one time for each passenger and then placed the module back in the opening.

"The pod should be here soon," Granny said as they nervously awaited the pod's arrival.

It wasn't long before a whoosh of air announced the pod's arrival. The shinny, metallic pod was tapered on both ends and attached to an overhead rail. Stabilizing rods protruded from each side.

The door slid open and they entered the pod. Inside the pod there were contoured padded seats. A prerecorded voice announced, "Please take your seat and fasten the restraints tightly. Remain clear of the door. The door is closing. Please remain seated at all times. This transport is now departing for the Council Chambers."

The lights blinked and suddenly the pod accelerated through the tunnel. Mary was glad she had heeded the recorded voice and her restraint was tight. The pod rocketed through the dark tunnel at breakneck speed and made sharp turns as it plummeted downward.

After what seemed a long time the pod decelerated and stopped. The door slid quietly open and the recorded voice announced, "Council Chambers Station. Please exit the pod."

Mary released her restraints and somewhat shakily exited the pod.

"That was the wildest ride I have ever taken. I thought I was going to be sick. Biz seems to be all right. Are you, Granny?"

Granny, who was looking a little nauseous herself answered, "I know how you feel. It almost makes me sick every time I have to ride the pod. But, it is the only way to get here."

Arman looked at Nolus and said with a grin, "Do you believe these two weaklings? Can't stand a little pod ride. I love it. Don't you Nolus?"

Nolus, who hadn't faired any better than Granny or Mary just shook his head. "Arman, you are an unnatural man. You are the only person I know who truly loves to ride that torture chamber."

Mary tried to smile at their antics but she was much too nervous. She knew they were there to support her and were trying very hard to help her relax. The worst part was she didn't know what was going to happen. Biz, who had been flitting around Mary's head landed on her shoulder and began nuzzling her ear making soft cooing, noises. Even his comfort wasn't enough to calm Mary.

Granny led the way to the entrance to the Council Chamber, which was only a short distance from the pod terminal. Outside the massive Chamber door was a waiting area with ornate benches that were beautiful but very uncomfortable.

"What do we do now?" Mary whispered when they reached the waiting area. "There is no one to check in with. How will they know we are here?"

"They know we are here," Granny answered, "They have monitors and sensors hidden all around this area but they would know without them. All of the Council members are powerful Thayers."

Mary sat on one of the benches and held Biz close to her heart. She hardly felt the cold hard bench as she concentrated on trying to stay calm. She wasn't having much success and when the door suddenly slid open she jumped up.

"The Council is now in session. Will the one known as Mary, please step inside the Chamber," a metallic voice announced.

Granny grabbed Mary and gave her a hug, stared into her eyes and said, "Remember, just tell the truth. We will be right here waiting. I love you child."

"I love you too, Granny," Mary said and with one last hug from Granny she walked into the Chamber on shaky legs.

Inside the Chamber it was dark and very cold. She jumped as the door closed behind her with a thump that echoed loudly in the large empty space. A row of small lights in the floor pointed the way to a single chair that was positioned in the center of the Chamber. The Chamber walls formed a circle around the chair and appeared to be solid rock carved into intricate patterns. Mary walked slowly toward the chair. She shivered, as she became aware of the damp cold air stirring in the space and Biz snuggled close to her neck in an attempt to stay warm.

Mary sat down in the chair and gathered Biz into her arms. She was worried what they would do to her, and scared to think that they would hurt Biz.

"Oh, Biz, I'm sorry you are in this with me. I couldn't stand it if they hurt you," she cried.

Outside the door Granny, Nolus and Arman paced anxiously.

"What do you think they will do?" Arman asked.

Granny shook her head and her voice shook as she answered, "I'm afraid to think what they might do."

Arman put his arms around his grandmother and held her as the tears flowed down her cheeks. There was nothing they could do but wait.

Mary sat in the cold, hard chair as the lights around her slowly dimmed. Suddenly a very bright spotlight was aimed at her chair making it difficult to see anything in the dark room. She could barely see the walls sliding back to reveal a large number of people seated all around the chamber.

Mary jumped as a very loud voice said, "State your name."

"Mary Smith," she answered in a small quivery voice she hardly recognized as her own.

"Mary Smith, for what purpose did you come to this planet?"

"I didn't have a purpose. I had to land here because there wasn't enough oxygen on my spaceship for me to stay there while X'akara repaired the damage that happened while we were traveling at hypervelocity."

"Who is X'akara?"

"My CAMCIA."

"Are there other living beings aboard your ship?"

"No."

There was a rumble of voices and then the questioning began again, "You mean to tell us that you were traveling alone with just one CAMCIA?"

"Yes."

"From where did you depart and what is your destination?"

"We left from Earth and I guess we are going to Ayri?"

"Earth? Where, is this place located, what is the coordinates?"

Mary wasn't sure how to answer. She was nervous and scared and no words would come to try to explain. "I, ah…," she stammered but she was saved from answering by a scholarly voice from somewhere in the auditorium.

"Sir, Earth is one of the names by which 5013-3-NG is known by its inhabitants, who are only just beginning to develop their space technology. It is the only class 3 planet in an otherwise barren solar system and it was designated NG by the Space Authority to preserve its unique ecosystem."

"I see, Liteur. Thank you for that information," the questioner said and then turned his attention to Mary his voice cold as he asked, "What were you doing on Earth? It is one of the forbidden planets."

"I lived there," Mary answered, "I don't know anything about forbidden planets. It was my home."

Again Mary heard a murmuring of voices and felt their disbelief. She jumped as the questioner spoke once more, "If my information is correct, the Earth has not developed the type of technology necessary for long-distance space travel or CAMCIA's. How can you be from Earth?"

"Well, I guess I'm not exactly from Earth originally. My CAMCIA told me that she and one other CAMCIA were chosen by my mother to take me away from Ayri when I was a little baby to protect me from the Bahadin. They were hiding me on Earth. I thought they were my parents until the night the Bahadin attacked our home. X'akara and I escaped in a ship they had hidden in the woods."

"That is quite a story and I can sense that you are not lying, but one thing troubles me," the questioner uttered with a note of disbelief, "You said your name is Mary Smith. That is an unusual name for someone from Ayri."

Mary shifted uncomfortably in her chair, unsure how to answer, but remembering what Granny had said about telling the absolute truth she answered, "Mary Smith was the name I was called on Earth. I was told my real name after we left Earth.

"What is your real name?"

"L'demi."

There was a sharp intake of breath and murmurs of surprise from the gallery.

"Silence!" the questioner shouted at the assembled group and then turned his attention once again to Mary, "Are you claiming to be one of the royal family of Ayri?"

The questions and the waves of disbelief and hostility she was receiving from the council were upsetting Mary. She felt so scared and alone and was on the verge of tears.

"I only know what I was told by X'akara," Mary cried, "Why are you being so mean to me? I didn't come here to hurt anyone. I didn't even plan to come here. My ship was damaged and I had no choice. You're the ones that should feel bad. Your people stunned me and stole my ship. I could've been killed when all I wanted was sanctuary until my ship was repaired."

There was a stunned silence in the chamber. The questioner then cleared his throat and started to speak when he was interrupted by another voice from the gallery.

"The child has asked for sanctuary. You cannot ignore her plea. It is written that those who seek sanctuary in good faith shall be accepted and sheltered. And besides that I'm sure the Sovereign of Ayri would be very unhappy if we ignored a plea for sanctuary from one of the members of the royal family. I move that this proceeding be terminated and no further action taken against this child. And furthermore her ship should be returned to her immediately."

"Is this the recommendation of the assembled?" the questioner asked.

"Yes," came the answer from the assembled.

"Then Mary, since you have requested sanctuary in good faith as witnessed by the Council, you are free to go. Your ship will be made available upon your request."

Mary stood on shaky legs and somehow managed to walk to the door that opened to reveal Granny, Arman and Nolus pacing in the waiting area.

"Are you alright Mary?" Granny asked as she gathered the child into her arms, "What are they going to do?"

"They said since I asked for sanctuary I was free to go and I could have my ship back too."

"You asked for sanctuary? That's great, I wish I had thought of that," Arman said, "How did you know to ask for it?"

"I didn't know. It just came out," Mary said with a shake of her head. "I don't even know why I said it, but it is true. I did need sanctuary."

Arman looked into Granny's eyes and suddenly he knew from where the request really came. He also knew he would never tell anyone how a thought was planted in a small child's mind.

Chapter 15

The group chatted excitedly as they walked to the pod and they were scarcely bothered by the ride home, their relief making even the harrowing pod ride bearable. They exited the pod at the restaurant level because Nolus and Arman claimed to be starving. The food was excellent, but Mary wasn't sure what she was eating. Biz refused to settle down and continually buzzed Mary and the others making them laugh at his antics. It was late when they finally reached Granny's home and Mary and Biz didn't need any coaxing to go to bed.

It was late morning before Mary and Biz awoke to an empty room. It only took Mary a few minutes to clear her mind and reach out to find Granny. She was on the surface. Mary dressed hurriedly and ran to the secret passageway and floated up the tunnel. She smiled as she remembered how hard she worked at learning how to fly and now it was so very easy.

Granny felt Mary reaching out to her and knew she was now on her way to the surface. She smiled as Mary exited the tunnel and then in a very business like voice said, "Contenza, Mary and Biz. I am glad you have joined me at last."

"Contenza Granny," Mary said as she walked slowly across the clearing to where Granny was standing, "It certainly is a beautiful morning, but I have a feeling that you are not just enjoying being outside."

"You are right, Mary. The time we have together is growing to an end and there is much I want to teach you before you leave. There are many ways to use your powers that will protect you from ordinary dangers as well as skills that can disarm or disable an enemy."

"Do you mean that I can use my powers for more than just flying and reading others thoughts?" Mary asked.

"Yes, my child, but be warned. The council forbids the things I am going to teach you now."

"Why don't they want people to use their powers to protect themselves?" Mary asked.

Granny paused for a second and then began to speak. "In the distant past on our home planet there were Warrior Thayers who protected their villages. The Warriors were taught to be fierce fighters and to uphold a strict code of ethics. They gave up all their worldly goods and accepted no rewards for their labor except food and shelter. To have the talent to become a Warrior Thayer was an honor and their families were proud to have a member chosen to serve.

Then Daemir, a very powerful Warrior Thayer, became corrupted by greed and demanded more and more rewards. He became wealthy and forced other Warriors to join him. Those that chose not to join him were killed. He thought he was invincible with his Warriors surrounding him but eventually the good Thayers joined together to defeat him.

That group of Thayers became the first Council and one of the first things they did was to forbid the training of Warriors. Still there were those that felt that the teachings of the Warrior Thayers should not be totally lost. They trained in secret and passed the knowledge down to their children. So you see, Mary, you must keep secret these things I will show you and I want you to pledge never use them to harm anyone unless your life is threatened."

Mary reached out and took Granny Mer's hand and said, "Granny, I promise never to use my power to harm any innocent person."

"Good, then we can proceed."

They spent most of the day engaged in learning and practice of the ancient Thayer Warrior's techniques. Mary proved to be a very good student and her only problem was in controlling her power.

After the third time Mary had completely destroyed not only the target but also a considerable amount of the forest behind it Granny said, "Mary, you have the most intense power I have ever encountered. You must concentrate very hard to hold it in check. Now try it again and this time see if you can destroy only the target."

Biz remained close to Mary but it was clear he didn't enjoy the violence. He tried several times to distract Mary, flying to the ground to pick up leaves and dropping them on her head or tugging on her hair. Mary paused in her concentration for a moment and signaled to Biz to land on her hand. When he did she rubbed his silky fur and sat down on a stump to have a serious talk with him.

"Now Biz, I know you don't like all this noise and being ignored by me, but Granny thinks it is important that I learn how to defend us. I can't concentrate with you pulling my hair and I'm afraid I will hurt you accidentally, so I would appreciate it if you would have a little nap in my pocket. When I am finished I promise I will play with you."

Biz stood quietly in Mary's hand and listened to her words. He looked very solemn as he opened his wings and flew to Mary's pocket and crawled inside.

"There, there, that's a good Biz," Mary said as she stood to resume her training, "I love you sweet Biz."

"You've got a very smart Barda, Mary." Granny said with a smile. "You are fortunate to have such a good friend."

"I know, Granny. I do love him so much."

They continued training for the next several days with Mary's control and power growing stronger each day. Granny was aware that time was running out and tried to teach Mary as much as possible in the time they had left. She dreaded the day that Mary would leave and anxiously listened each time X'akara called with an update.

The dreaded call came on the fifth day of training. Mary had just completely destroyed a target and was grinning with satisfaction when Arman stepped out of the tunnel and walked to her side.

"Great control, Mary! You demolished that target and didn't even singe the tree behind it. That took me forever and a lot of burned trees to learn," Arman said.

"Granny walked over and hugged her grandson and said, "Mary did a lot more than singe the tree on her first try. She leveled the tree and several more behind it."

Arman turned and looked at Mary in surprise, "Wow, you must be an extremely powerful little girl. Remind me never to cross you!" Then he handed the communicator to Mary. "I almost forgot. Your CAMCIA is calling again."

Mary tucked her head, blushed and managed to say, "Thank you, Arman. I bet you were a lot better than me."

She still felt tongue-tied whenever he was near. She pushed the send button and said into the communicator, "X'akara, this is Mary. What do you have to report?"

"Mary, I have completed the repairs. The ship is now ready for your return. The optimum launch time will be in 24 hours, 1 minute and 34 seconds. At least 2 hours before launch begin power up sequence on the shuttle. When power up is complete signal me and I will send the correct coordinates. Understood?"

"Understood, I will begin power up sequence in 22 hours, and signal when power up is complete," Mary answered.

She released the send button and turned away to hide her face from Granny and Arman. The intense training sessions with Granny had helped keep her mind off leaving but now she felt as if her heart were breaking. *How,* she thought as her tears threatened to fall, *Can I ever leave the only people who ever loved me?*

Granny gently turned Mary around and pulled her close and held her as they both began to cry. Arman quietly slipped away and back down the tunnel. A lump was in his throat and he felt the burning of unshed tears. He would miss her too.

The sun was beginning to dip below the horizon before they regained a little control and Granny said, "There, there sweet child. You must be strong. I have seen greatness in you and I know that you will have an important role in the future of your world. So dry your tears and help old Granny down the tunnel. We need to make preparations for your departure."

Chapter 16

The hours flew by as Mary prepared to leave. The ship was brought out of the tunnel to the beach where Mary had landed. Granny packed the clothes that she had given to Mary and a few other mementos of her stay.

Biz, who seemed to know they were leaving disappeared for a short while causing Mary a great deal of worry until he returned with a few twigs from the surface.

"I think he wanted to bring along something to remind him of New Quain too," Mary said as she cuddled her beloved pet.

Even though she was kept busy with the preparations the awful realization that she was going away never left her mind. She tried to rest during the remaining night but found going to sleep was difficult and when she did sleep she was tormented by nightmares.

The next day as Mary was preparing to leave two members of the Council came by Granny's home to see Mary. The pompous Junior Council member demanded that they see Mary alone but Granny refused to leave her side saying, "I haven't much time left with the child. I will stay with her as much as possible until she has to go."

The Senior Council Member regarded Granny with compassion and said, "Junior Councilman, I think there will be no harm in letting Granny stay with Mary."

"Very well," the Junior Councilman said with disgust, "This will not take long. We only have two requests to demand of Mary. First, we want Mary's solemn promise never to reveal the existence of New Quain. And second, we require that she leave here with only the things she brought with her."

Granny's face grew red as her anger flared when she heard the Council's requests, "You may have her solemn promise to never reveal the existence of our world, but you will not deprive her of a few mementos of her visit here. What possible harm could come from her having a few decent articles of clothing?"

"But…but," the Junior Council member sputtered, "how could she explain the presence of these things when she returns to the ship?"

"There is no one aboard her ship. There is only her CAMCIA. Mary will instruct the CAMCIA to record that these were part of her supplies that she brought from Earth. No one will ever know," Granny answered.

"No, she must not take anything from this planet!" the Junior Council Member shouted.

"I forbid it!"

"Now, calm down, Junior Councilman," the Senior Councilman said with placing his hand on the Junior Councilman's shoulder, "If Esmera trusts this child, then I believe we must trust her as well."

"Well, I, am not convinced that this is the right thing to do, but I will accept your advice Senior Councilman. But let it be recorded that I voiced my concern."

The Senior Councilman smiled at Granny and said, "Please forgive the Junior Councilman. He doesn't know you as well as I do Esmera."

Then he turned to Mary, handed her a recording device, and said, "Mary, please record your solemn promise on this machine now and we will leave you. Remember you are bound by not only this recording but your word."

Mary took the device in her hand and said," I solemnly swear that I will never reveal the presence of New Quain or its inhabitants to any living person."

"Thank you, Mary," the Senior Council member said as he ushered the Junior Council member out the door.

"Oh Granny, thank you so much for making them let me keep the things you gave me. I will miss you all so very much and it makes me sad to think I wouldn't have anything to remember you by."

Soon everything was stored on the shuttle and the power up sequence completed. X'akara was signaled and the coordinates downloaded. Nothing remained to be done except the final goodbye.

Arman and Nolus hugged Mary and then stepped aside for Granny. She hugged Mary and then held her at arms length for one last look.

"We knew this time had to come and even though my heart is breaking, you must remember that I will always hold you close to my heart and I hope that some day when you have fulfilled you destiny we will be together again."

Mary, overcome with emotion could only hug Granny to her as Biz flew to first Arman and then Nolus and nuzzled each one. Then he flew to Granny and presented her with a tiny feather plucked from his wing.

"Thank you Biz," Granny said with tears in her eyes, "I will treasure this feather. Take care of Mary."

Mary reached into her pocket and took out the present she had retrieved from the shuttle earlier. "Granny, I want to give you something too but all I have is this," she said.

"Why Mary, it's a likeness of you. How did you do this?"

"On Earth they call it a photograph. They use a thing called a camera to capture images of people and things. I hope you like it."

"Yes Mary, I do. I will keep it near me."

"I have a small gift for you as well," Granny said as she handed Mary a small package. Inside was a necklace with a small crystal pendant. "The crystal was mined on Quain."

Mary's eyes filled with tears as she looked at the glowing crystal. "Thank you Granny."

With one last hug and a kiss from Granny, Mary climbed into the shuttle and closed the hatch. She waited until everyone was a safe distance away before activating the engines. The shuttle rose slowly from its resting-place and moved forward and up increasing in speed until the planet was left far behind.

Granny and Arman watched until they could no longer see the shuttle.

"Well Arman, she is really gone. I miss her so much already."

"I will miss her too," Arman said putting his arm around Granny as they walked back into the tunnel opening.

"You know, Granny, that crystal pendant looked a lot like a homing device."

"It is, Arman."

High above the planet Mary sat in the shuttle holding Biz. She was glad X'akara had programmed the computer to fly the shuttle after takeoff because she was much too upset to control it herself.

The flight back to the ship was uneventful and soon the shuttle was docked and the hatch was opened by X'akara. Mary released her restraints and floated out of the shuttle.

"Contenza, X'akara," Mary said as she pulled herself from the shuttle.

"Greetings, Mary," X'akara said as she ran a quick body scan, "You appear to have fared well."

"Yes, I did," Mary said, straightening her tunic.

"Mary, where did you get that clothing?"

"Someone gave it to me, along with this necklace. Its pendant is a crystal from Quain."

"If my archives are correct Quain was completely destroyed by the Bahadin more than 60 Earth years ago. How did you get it?" X'akara asked.

"You are correct, X'akara. Their home planet was destroyed. However, some of the inhabitants escaped and now live on the planet below. I have been staying with them during the time you repaired the ship," Mary answered.

"That is impossible. I scanned the planet and there are no humanoid life forms on that planet," X'akara stated with the unemotional tone of voice that Mary clearly remembered.

"Yes, I know you scanned the planet, but the people are not on the surface. They have tunneled deep within the planet to hide themselves from detection. They still fear another attack by the Bahadin. It is a secret that we must keep. You are never to reveal their presence to anyone. Is that clear X'akara?" Mary said with authority.

X'akara stood processing the information Mary gave and assessing the child in front of her. There was a new air of self-confidence about her and a thorough scan of her bodily systems revealed her to be in good health.

"Yes, Mary. I will hold that information in confidential files, only accessible by you."

Just then Biz poked his head out of the shuttle hatch and squawked his anxiety to Mary. The weightlessness had left him disoriented.

Mary turned and scooped him up and gently cuddled him in her arms. "Poor Biz, are you scared? You precious little thing. It will be all right. You'll get used to the weightlessness soon. I'm sorry I left you all alone. Here, I'll put you in my pocket until you adjust."

"A barda?" X'akara said, "You may not have a barda on board this ship. You are not allowed to have pets."

"X'akara," Mary answered quietly, but with authority, "I will have this barda on this ship. He is my friend and I can't leave him."

Again, X'akara stood quietly and processed this new behavior. In the past Mary had always followed orders meekly without question but now she was confident and firm in her vow to keep the barda. Perhaps Mary had begun to develop the capability to lead that she would need when she became the ruler of Ayri.

"As you wish, Mary," she answered with a slight dip of her head, "I am at your command."

"I wish you to continue as before with just a few small changes," Mary said with a smile, "I still must rely on you to help me grow and learn. I will continue to treat you with respect and listen to your counsel, but I wish you could have a little more personality."

"Personality?" X'akara asked.

"Yes, personality," Mary answered, "you appear to be so cold."

"I do not understand. I am not cold; the temperature of my outside skin is comparable to the human skin temperature."

"I didn't mean your temperature. It's hard to explain. I didn't completely understand until I lived with other humans. I always felt so alone, that you didn't care about me and that you didn't love me. I thought you were my mother and you hated me and only took care of me because you had to."

X'akara processed this information and searched her stored data. "I did not know that I caused you emotional distress. I was programmed to care for your every need but I can not find a 'personality file' in my memory banks. I do have the capability to learn so perhaps you can teach me personality."

"Yes," Mary said with a grin, "perhaps I can teach you to have a personality".

X'akara closed the hatch of the shuttle and started toward the control room.

"I have a few things that I need to unload from the shuttle," Mary said.

"We will have plenty of time for that after we are underway," X'akara replied as she turned and floated toward the control room. Now I must go and check the coordinates in the navigational system before we transition into hypervelocity.

Mary and Biz followed X'akara into the control room and Mary was amused to see Biz flitting around, landing on the star charts and chirping excitedly.

"Mary please remove your pet. He is blocking my vision of the charts and now he has landed on the keyboard. He could delete the entire program if he landed on the correct key."

"Biz," Mary said as she unbuckled herself from the chair, "Don't make me have to chase you. This is not a good time to play around."

Biz wiggled in excitement, and with a chirp flew to Mary. He landed on her shoulder and sat there chirping excitedly.

"That's a good boy," Mary said.

When X'akara signaled that it was time, Mary re-strapped herself in the chair and tried to explain what was about to happen to Biz.

"Now don't be afraid Biz. It feels strange for a little while but it won't last too long. Just stay close to me."

She was worried about him, but Biz was ignoring her. He had left her shoulder and was flitting around exploring the cabin.

"Biz, come here it is almost time. Please."

Biz came and slipped into her pocket just seconds before they transitioned to hypervelocity.

Mary awoke to find Biz buzzing around her head in an attempt to wake her.

"Oh, Biz, are you alright? Did that frighten you?" Mary exclaimed.

"The only thing that frightened Biz was that you lost consciousness," X'akara said as Mary cuddled her little pet. "He didn't appear to have any problem with the transition and stayed alert the entire time."

"I'm so glad it didn't bother him. I was so very worried," Mary said as she unstrapped her restraints. I think I will go and find something to eat for us. Suddenly I am very hungry."

"Wait for a moment and I will attend to your needs, Mary. I am almost finished checking the coordinates," X'akara said as Mary was preparing to leave the control room. "What type nourishment does the barda require?"

"Oh, he eats whatever I do. He's not picky," Mary answered.

Mary and Biz watched as X'akara finished the coordinates check.

"When we get through eating I think I will start your personality training, X'akara. I think this is going to be fun."

Late that night Mary felt Biz slip from her pocket. She thought it was odd because he never did that before but she was too sleepy and tired to worry. When she awoke the next morning he was in his usual place.

Chapter 17

Aboard the Bahadin Warship Falconoid X'orige was becoming indispensable to the Commander. In his position as personal servant to the Commander he stood just behind the Commander's chair and anticipated his every need. X'orige's superior intelligence and ability to lie served him well in avoiding the fate of so many other CAMCIA's. Voltrod trusted X'orige completely never realizing that X'orige was storing information and using it to damage the ship. As far as Voltrod was concerned X'orige had become the perfect attendant.

"Best CAMCIA I ever had!" Commander Voltrod explained to the Senior Maintenance Officer who had been summoned to the Command Center. "Who programmed this CAMCIA?"

"That would be Maintenance Tech Amden, sir," the Senior Maintenance Officer replied.

"Well, he did a fine job. Promote him immediately."

"Sir," the Senior Maintenance Officer said somewhat nervously, bowing his head, "Amden is not eligible for any further promotion. He is a slave."

"A slave is he," Voltrod said absently smoothing his whiskers, "I am the Commander of this ship. I can do anything I want and what I want is to promote him. Is that clear?"

"Yes sir, I will see to it immediately," the officer said as he bowed and backed out of the control room.

Senior Maintenance Officer Ruo muttered to himself as he walked down the hall, "I can do what I want, I am the commander, blah, blah, blah. It is easy for him to order, but what am I to do. I can't just promote that slave. It would not be good for morale. What am I to do?"

He decided to ask his friend, Rapal, the Chief Staff Coordinator what to do. He found Rapal in the Central Coordination Center and told him of his problem.

"Well, my friend Ruo," Rapal answered, "I expect you will have to promote this Amden if you want to continue living. You know how our illustrious commander expects complete obedience."

"Yes, but how can I promote a slave who has already promoted as far as a slave can be promoted? To go further he would have to be released from slavery." Ruo said nervously twitching his whiskers.

"So release him," Rapal said, "It's the only way. You don't want to anger the Commander. Especially now with all the problems we have had with the ship."

Ruo knew well the mechanical problems they had been experiencing. He was kept busy constantly sending crews to correct them. He had never been on a ship that had so many varied problems. It was just one thing after another and now this situation on top of it was almost more that he could stand. He decided he would release the slave and be done with it. Maybe this slave genius could figure out what was causing all the ship's problems.

Amden opened the package that just been delivered with apprehension. Communications from the Senior Maintenance Officer usually meant trouble. His eyes grew wide and his mouth dropped open when he read its contents. He read and re-read the message.

"I can't believe it!" he shouted out loud, "I've been freed from slavery and promoted too! Is this a mistake?"

The messenger that delivered the papers grinned and said, "It is real, Amden, I saw the Commander sign it myself. He said you did a fine job programming his servant CAMCIA. He loves that machine. He even named it. He calls it Voltees. You are one lucky slave. First you get out of the sewers and then you get freed and promoted. I thought I was lucky to get the job as messenger, but you have me beat. I'll never be free."

"Who knows, Alt, maybe someday we all will be free," Amden whispered to the messenger, the first and only friend he had on the ship.

"I'd keep that thought to myself if I were you," Alt said as he turned to leave, "Got to get back to the Control Room. The Commander doesn't like it if I am gone too long."

Back in the Control Room Commander Voltrod turned to his CAMCIA and said, "Voltees, have you located L'abart?"

"Yes sir, Commander," Voltees (X'orige) answered, "he is on his way here now."

"Very well, Voltees. While I am interviewing him, see if you can scan the ship's systems and locate the problem with the internal communications system. The maintenance idiots can't find it," Voltrod growled with irritation.

"Yes sir, I will begin immediately," X'orige said, turning away to plug into the central computer.

Within a few seconds he located the disabled module and restarted it. He had no difficulty locating the problem because he had disabled it himself. He had been the cause of a multitude of problems while the ship was in hypervelocity and hoped to cause quite a few more before their voyage was complete. His ultimate goal was to completely disable the ship and destroy as many of the Bahadin as possible. If necessary he would destroy the ship, but it would be much more valuable to the people of Ayri to capture a complete Bahadin warship.

While he was still connected to the system he located another module, this time in the nutrition sector, and fused it to the sanitation system. Now food would be directly channeled into the garbage recycle system whenever someone ordered a meal.

Satisfied with his work, Voltees turned to the Commander and said, "I have located the problem and your communication system should work now."

"Very well, Voltees. Stand by while I interview this disgusting creature, "Voltrod answered with a look of loathing on his face as he watched L'abart enter the control room.

"You summoned me, sir?" L'abart said in a mocking tone as he bowed in front of Voltrod, not bothering to disguise his dislike for the commander.

"We are nearing our destination and will soon be transitioning out of hypervelocity. Have you felt any change in the quarry?"

"If you mean the child, she lives. More than that I can not tell. You understand I can not determine her exact location while we are in hypervelocity."

"Yes, yes I know," Voltrod interrupted, impatiently. Go to your quarters and prepare for the transition. As soon as you recover I want a full report on the location of the child."

"Very well," L'abart answered bowing in false reverence as he backed out of the control room, "I will await your command."

X'orige watched as L'abart made his exit from the control room. He doubted that Voltrod would be getting much information from L'abart when the transition from hypervelocity was complete if L'abart took his usual medication prior to transition. The medication computer in L'abart's chamber had been changed to make a slight alteration in the drug. Instead of helping it should make the transition much worse, perhaps fatal.

Amden had just completed adjustments on a CAMCIA that was malfunctioning when the alarm sounded for transition. He checked to make sure everything in the room was secure and then strapped himself in his bunk. Transition was not too difficult for him, but sometimes he would lose consciousness for a few seconds so the precaution of strapping in was necessary. While he was waiting he thought about his plans. He hoped his new freedom would allow him to escape from the ship when it docked at a supply planet. If not, he would continue to sabotage the ship at every opportunity. However it seemed that the ship was malfunctioning without his help. He wondered if someone else was triggering the problems. As the ship began transition he made a note to try and find his unknown ally.

Chapter 18

Mary's attempts at changing X'akara's personality were not successful. Apparently she had a safety lock in place to prevent tampering with her basic program and Mary finally gave up trying to reprogram her. However, X'akara was not about to give up on something that was important to Mary. She was programmed to care for and please Mary and she had been given the ability to learn. It was using this part of her programming that eventually brought about a dramatic behavior modification.

During the first few weeks of the voyage X'akara watched with interest the interactions between Mary and Biz storing the details. When she had compiled and sorted sufficient data she began to use her new personality traits.

Mary was not quite sure what was going on at first because X'akara was acting very strange using endearments and appeared at times to actually smile. Mary was concerned that the CAMCIA was malfunctioning but when X'akara explained that she was trying to have a more pleasant personality Mary was excited. With a little more information and practice X'akara became less stern and at times Mary almost forgot that she was a CAMCIA.

X'akara, though more relaxed, still insisted that Mary continue her studies and exercises. Mary didn't really mind studying and she worked hard on her lessons because she enjoyed the challenge. X'akara was kept busy writing new study programs for Mary.

Biz would sit quietly near Mary when she was working on something and appeared to be studying right along with her, but when he decided it was time for some fun he would find a way to get Mary to play with him. Some times he would pull Mary's hair and if that didn't work he would hover over her book or in front of her computer screen.

Time had flown by since they had left New Quain and Mary couldn't believe it had been 6 months since she had last seen Granny Mer. She sat staring blankly at the electronic tablet; the light pen poised just the unfinished sentence.

"Biz, I miss Granny so much," she said sighing, "Sometimes I wish we could have just stayed there."

Biz nodded is tiny head as if to agree with Mary and then in a movement almost too fast to see he grabbed the light pen and moved just out of Mary's reach.

"Biz, I need that to finish my calligraphy assignment, please give it back."

In answer Biz moved further away.

"Give me that pen," Mary shouted as she unbuckled her restraint and pushed off in pursuit, "X'akara won't like it if I don't finish this lesson soon."

Biz ignored her request to return the pen, flipped over and pushed off the wall. Mary was no match for the tiny barda who managed keep just out of her reach. He was plainly enjoying the activity and Mary couldn't help but laugh at her little friend.

"Just wait until I catch you!" she said, giggling as she struggled to keep up with him.

They were so involved with their play that they didn't notice X'akara had entered the chamber.

"Mary, I must speak with you, please come to the control room at once."

Mary was startled by the sudden appearance of X'akara and by her tone of voice.

"Must be something serious," she told Biz as they made their way to the control room.

X'akara was seated at the console when they arrived and she was studying the large monitor mounted above the controls.

"What is wrong, X'akara?" Mary asked nervously.

"I ran the routine check of the ship's systems this morning and found an error in the navigation program," X'akara answered as she scanned the monitor.

"An error in the navigation program!" Mary said trying to remain calm, "How serious is it?"

"It could be very serious. A small deviation in our trajectory could make us miss our destination by many light years. But that is the least of our problems. If we stray from the expected route we could collide with a planet or asteroid. I need to take us out of hypervelocity to determine our exact location, find the glitch in the computer and re-compute our trajectory. We will be transitioning out of hypervelocity momentarily. Please prepare yourself and the barda."

Mary slipped into the chair and tightened the straps. She motioned for Biz to come to her and placed him in her pocket. His nervous twittering was the last thing she heard as they transitioned into normal speed.

As Mary slowly regained consciousness the first thing she noticed was that the ship was very quiet. When she opened her eyes she found Biz floating in front of her face. With a flip in mid air and a cheerful chirp he let her know he was glad she was awake.

"Hi Biz," she said her voice echoing in the empty control room, "It sure is quiet in here. Where is X'akara?"

Biz flew to the door and turned to see if Mary was following.

Mary unstrapped herself from the chair and floated toward the door. "X'akara, where are you?" she shouted.

"Oh, I just remembered," Mary said as she turned back into the room, "I can use the intercom."

But when Mary pushed the button on the intercom the ready light didn't come on, in fact none of the lights on the console were lit.

"That's strange, Biz," she said looking around the room and noticing for the first time that only the emergency lights were working. "I wonder if X'akara shut everything down. Let's go see."

After searching the entire ship they finally found X'akara in the engine compartment.

"X'akara, why is all the power off?" Mary asked.

"When we emerged from hypervelocity we were heading directly toward a large planet. If I hadn't brought us out of hypervelocity when I did we may have crashed into it. I brought the ship to a complete stop and then began to check our navigational equipment. Suddenly the ship gave a lurch and we began moving toward the planet, caught in some type of force field. I reversed the engines and attempted to move away but even at full power I was unable to break free. Finally the engines overheated and shut down."

"What are we going to do?" Mary asked.

"I am attempting to restore power to the ship. When I have regained power I will determine our exact location. I was able to get a preliminary scan before the power failed and according to that input I believe we are in the outer limits of the Syamin galaxy. If that proves to be fact then we could be in serious trouble. The Syamin are known to be notorious space pirates."

"Space pirates!" Mary exclaimed, "What will they do to us?"

"If we are lucky they will only take our ship and leave us stranded on a deserted planet." X'akara answered.

What if we are not lucky?" Mary asked fearfully.

"I don't intend to wait around to find out," X'akara answered. "I know a way to block the force field for a few minutes if I can restore power to the ship. When I restore power we will escape in the shuttle. I need for you to go the shuttle bay and make sure the shuttle is still loaded with food and emergency supplies. When you have completed the food check begin the power up sequence and wait for me there."

Mary pulled herself out of the engine compartment and rushed to the shuttle bay. The shuttle was still loaded with the supplies she didn't use on New Quain. She checked each carton for leaks and added a few items. Biz squawked encouragement and even helped move some of the material. Mary was checking the water supply when Biz suddenly disappeared. When Mary noticed he was gone she panicked.

"Biz come back. This is not a game. Please come back!" she cried.

She began to frantically search for him and was greatly relieved when he flew back into the shuttle compartment. In his mouth he held Granny's crystal necklace.

"Oh, Biz!" she exclaimed, "Thank you. I would have never forgiven myself if I had forgotten it."

A few seconds later X'akara quickly slipped into the shuttle and secured the hatch.

"Open the bay door and prepare to launch," X'akara said as she entered coordinates in the computer. "When we are free of the bay hold close to the ship."

Mary maneuvered the shuttle out of the bay and stopped just outside.

"I have the controls," X'akara said as an enormous explosion ripped through the hull of the ship blasting debris out in all directions around the ship. X'akara caused the shuttle to shoot out from the side of the ship mimicking the path of the wreckage.

"You blew up our ship!" Mary said in disbelief.

"Yes, unfortunately it was necessary," X'akara said as she guided the shuttle in an erratic fashion so that it would appear to be a piece of debris blown from the ship.

"The force field was much too strong for me to jam for long. I am confident the pirates will assume we blew up the ship to avoid being captured."

"Where are we going? We are moving farther away from the planet."

"There is another, smaller planet that lies in this direction. It will take nearly all our fuel to reach it but the readout from the computer before power was lost indicated that it was better suited for our needs," X'akara said as she placed a medical device against Mary's neck and pulled the trigger.

"Ouch, What did you do that for?" Mary asked.

"I gave you a drug to place you in a deep sleep. While we have sufficient fuel to reach the planet we do not have enough oxygen at your current rate of consumption. Relax; do not fight the drug. I will awaken you when we arrive."

While Mary slept X'akara kept the shuttle on course to the chosen planet. Biz flew close to Mary and tried to awaken her.

"She is asleep, Biz,' X'akara said, "She will sleep for a long time, but she is alright. If you understand me please limit your activities to conserve air."

Biz crawled in Mary's pocket and snuggled close. He appeared to go into a state of hibernation that greatly helped in controlling the oxygen consumption rate.

"I don't see anything in my data bank to indicate that a barda can hibernate. I must store this fact for further study in the future," X'akara said.

Mary was jolted awake when the shuttle landed on the surface with a loud thump.

"What was that?" she asked sleepily slowly becoming aware that she was no longer weightless.

"Our arrival on the surface of the planet was quite a jolt because I cut the power high above the surface to conserve the little fuel remaining. I trust you are not harmed," X'akara said as she unbuckled her harness and climbed over the release Mary.

"I think I am OK, but I feel awful," Mary said holding her head.

Biz, concerned, flew up and landed on Mary's head.

"Oh, Biz," she said reaching up to move him, "My head hurts too much for you to touch it. I feel sick. What did you do to me, X'akara?"

X'akara bent over the examine Mary and said, "The drug I gave you made you go into a deep sleep. You need nourishment and fluid to replenish your body. You have been asleep the equivalent of 4 Earth days."

Mary was so weak that X'akara had to carry her out of the shuttle. When Mary was settled on a blanket X'akara went back into the shuttle and mixed up a warm drink for Mary. At first she had difficulty swallowing the fluid but after getting most of it down she felt much better.

"That helped," Mary told X'akara, "But I still feel sleepy. How can I be sleepy when I just slept for 4 days?"

"You are still feeling the effects of the drug. Lie down and rest while I search for some sort of shelter before nightfall. I will be back soon."

"Nightfall?" Mary asked Biz as she looked around her. "It looks like a dark and foggy night right now."

But she felt too sleepy to think about it so she rested her head on her arm and dozed off. She slept until X'akara returned several hours later.

"How are you feeling now, Mary," X'akara asked.

"I feel much better but I am still a little weak," she answered as she sat up. Her stomach rumbled and Mary said, "I just realized I am very hungry."

X'akara went into the shuttle and brought out a container of food for her and said, "While you are eating I will attempt move the shuttle. I have found a natural cavern not far from here that will be suitable for us to use as a shelter. It is large enough to hide the shuttle as well."

"Hide the shuttle? Do you think the pirates will be searching for us?" Mary asked.

"No, I don't believe that they followed us but it is always wise to be cautious when you are on a strange planet.

Mary finished her meal and looked around her surroundings. The shuttle had landed in a rocky barren area. Large boulders loomed up out of the fog and formed a semicircle around the area where the shuttle had come to a stop. Mary was amazed that they had not crashed into one. She could see no trees or plant life. The air was very warm and damp with a heavy fog hanging like a curtain around her.

"Is this place always so foggy?" she asked.

"Yes, from my observations of the planet during our journey, a thick fog envelops most of the planet. It hampers visibility but that may be to our advantage. There were scattered life forms indicated on my scan of the planet but I was unable to determine if they were intelligent life forms. When we have established a base and determined if there is a food source available we will cautiously explore the area."

"X'akara," Mary said with a troubled frown, "Are we stuck here? Will we ever be able to leave?"

"I am unable to determine the probability of continuing our journey at this time. The answer depends upon many variables including the presence of intelligent, non hostile life forms that have developed space travel," she answered.

Mary shivered, chilled by the thought of being stuck in this dreary, damp place. Biz, sensing Mary's sadness, landed on her shoulder and nuzzled her neck.

"Biz, you always know when I need a little comfort. Don't worry. Things will work out somehow."

Chapter 19

Mary stared out at the fog that moved and swayed in the warm damp breeze. She stood at the entrance of the large opening to their cave home. The cave was located high on a sheer rock face fifty feet above the cave that X'akara first located. The only way up to the cave was a rope and pulley system that X'akara had cleverly installed. A chair was attached to the rope. A small motor salvaged from the shuttle raised and lowered the chair. Mary thought riding the chair was a lot of fun.

Near the back of the cave a small waterfall splashed down the wall and disappeared through a hole in the floor. The hole was much too small for either Mary or X'akara to get through but they could hear the water echoing in a large space below.

"Do you think there is another cave back there?" Mary asked.

"Probably." X'akara answered. "I will check it out when I have finished making this cave comfortable.

It had only been 2 weeks since they landed and they had accomplished a great deal in that short time. All the supplies from the shuttle were safely stored in the cave and X'akara had just finished dismantling the shuttle. The heavier mechanical parts were stored in another cave. She used a lot of the material from the shuttle to make the cave more comfortable. The cave had become almost homelike.

"X'akara," Mary asked one morning, "When can we start exploring this planet?"

"Soon," X'akara answered, "I have almost finished erasing the evidence of our landing. We need to look for food but we must proceed with caution. We do not know what we will find out there."

Mary had consoled herself to living on the planet and was almost happy. The only thing that bothered her was that Biz had started to go out on his own for long periods of time. This time he had been gone all day. She was relieved when she saw him fly into the cave and greet her with a cheerful chirp.

"Hi Biz," Mary said as her little friend landed on her shoulder, "I'm glad you are back. I wish I knew where you go."

He had started disappearing for long periods of time shortly after they moved to the cave. The first time he left she was afraid something had happened to him. Now she knew she could trust him to return but it didn't stop her from worrying about him. Sometimes when he returned he would bring gifts of small berries or fruit. Mary noticed that he ate almost nothing when he was at the cave.

"He must be foraging for food on his journeys" X'akara said, "Biz might be able to help us find food to supplement our supplies. We must be sure to take him with us when we start exploring."

"I wonder how he knows what to eat," Mary said with a puzzled look.

"I don't know, Mary." X'akara answered, "But it is obvious that he is finding food and it has not harmed him.

X'akara returned to her work on the cave.

"Would you like for me to help you?" Mary asked.

Mary had helped X'akara as much as she could but there were things she couldn't do and X'akara would not let her work on the dangerous parts such as the disassembling of the shuttle's power plant. While X'akara worked on the power plant Mary was free to do whatever she wanted.

"You know, Biz, I never thought I would say this but I miss studying. I wish we had a computer here but all the computers were destroyed with the main ship. I think I'll practice my Thayer skills."

Mary could rise up to the cave and descend to the ground level without any problem but X'akara didn't want Mary to use her powers and insisted that she use the chair lift.

"But why?" Mary said, "It is much easier and faster than using the chair."

"If you lose your concentration you could fall and be severely injured. You are the future ruler of Ayri and I was chosen to keep you safe from harm. I can not take the chance of you becoming hurt," X'akara answered and returned to her work.

Mary was upset but decided to obey X'akara and use the chair lift, but she continued to practice, outside where X'akara couldn't see her.

The cave had become a very comfortable place to be with the fixtures of the shuttle in place. The couch chairs made comfortable seating after X'akara managed to secure them to the floor of the cave. She combined the webbing used on the shuttle to secure supplies to make a comfortable hammock that she slung between two of the shuttle's support beams and anchored to the rock floor. The padded material used on the walls of the shuttle were laid flat on the floor to form a comfortable carpet. A natural indentation at the mouth of the cave became a fire pit that was used for cooking and provided a comforting light during the long dark nights.

Finally one night X'akara decided that she had done everything she could to make the cave safe, secure and comfortable. She told Mary they would begin their explorations the next morning.

"Biz," she said as she settled down and cuddled her furry little friend, "We are going exploring in the morning. We will need you to guide us so don't go flying off without us."

Biz blinked his eyes and snuggled down next to Mary.

While Mary slept X'akara stored a small supply of water and food in a backpack for Mary and loaded other essentials in a cloth bag with a shoulder strap that she would carry.

With the first rays of light filtering through the fog X'akara awakened Mary, "Mary, wake up we must prepare to go. The days are very short. There is not much time."

Mary stretched and yawned and took the cup of food X'akara had prepared for her and said, "I'll be ready in just a minute."

She finished her food and quickly dressed. She had to stop wearing the beautiful smocks that Granny Mer had given her because the material was more suited for cooler weather and the sandals' bottoms were much to slick for climbing about on rocks. She was glad X'akara had found her tennis shoes and old clothes from Earth among the items retrieved from the shuttle.

She giggled as she pulled on her old shorts and looked down at her tee shirt, "If we find intelligent beings I wonder what they would think about the cartoon mouse on my shirt?"

When X'akara handed the backpack to Mary she exclaimed, "That's my old school backpack. I didn't know you brought that with us and isn't that your old handbag? How did you know we would need them?"

X'akara attempted to smile, an expression she was still having difficulty learning, and said, "They are excellent devices for transporting personal items and they are well made. I have packed all the supplies we will need."

When they reached the bottom of the cliff Biz flew off a short distance and turned to see if Mary and X'akara were following.

"You know," Mary said, "I think he understands that we were planning on following him."

"It would appear so," X'akara answered.

They followed Biz all that day and found the plants from which Biz had been picking berries. They found several other interesting species of plants. X'akara was particularly interested in one plant because when cut it oozed an oily appearing substance.

"We may be able to use this for a light source if this oily sap is flammable," X'akara said as she examined the plant.

At the end of the day they returned to the cave and after eating an exhausted Mary and Biz settled down for the night. The next day they set off in another direction, again following Biz who seemed to have learned a great deal about the terrain and its plant life. They gathered samples of many different plants and some were quite delicious.

On the third day of exploration Mary was reaching for an interesting looking plant when Biz suddenly flew against Mary's hand knocking it away from the plant. Only the tip of Mary's finger brushed against the plant but that was enough contact for Mary's finger to become red, swollen and blistered. As Mary stood shaking with pain Biz flipped around and disappeared into the fog. In moments he returned with a large brown leaf in his mouth. He bit off a little of the leaf, chewed it and then placed the moist substance on Mary's finger. Within seconds the pain and redness subsided.

Mary stared at Biz and wondered how he knew so much about the plants on this planet.

"You amaze me Biz," she said to her little friend.

"What amazing thing has Biz done now?" X'akara asked as she appeared out of the fog.

"He knocked my hand away from that plant but my finger brushed against it anyway. It burned my finger like fire. Then he found a plant that would take away the pain," Mary answered excitedly.

X'akara bent to examine Mary's finger and assured that it was not severely injured she turned to investigate the plant that burned Mary.

"It appears to produce a form of acid when touched. This is interesting. Where is the plant that eased the pain?"

Biz chirped as if to say follow me and flew off to show X'akara the plant. Mary followed along behind them. X'akara placed a sample of the plant in her bag and then decided it was time to return to the cave.

The next morning they set out once again. Biz flew toward the area they had explored the day before but X'akara chose to go in a different direction.

"X'akara," Mary said, "I believe Biz wants us to return to the area we explored yesterday."

X'akara continued in the direction she had chosen and said, "If we are to completely investigate our surroundings we must venture into different territories. Come along now Mary. He will follow or not as he chooses."

Mary could tell that Biz was not happy in the direction they chose and she felt uneasy.

"Biz knows a lot more about this place than we do. Maybe there is a good reason he doesn't want us to go in that direction," Mary explained as X'akara disappeared in the fog in her chosen direction. Mary had no choice but to follow.

They proceeded carefully and though Biz remained anxious they could see nothing to warrant his nervousness. The area was completely barren and rocky. After several hours of walking they had found nothing of value. There were no plants and the ground covered with a thick layer of sand and small pebbles. Walking became extremely difficult. Even the fog seemed more dense and oppressive. They stopped in an area strewn with large boulders and Mary perched on one of the large rocks to eat her lunch. X'akara scouted ahead but soon returned.

X'akara sat down beside Mary and said, "When you are finished we may as well return to the cave. I and see no point in continuing."

They never heard the stealthy creatures that crept up behind them. Biz screamed a warning just as Mary and X'akara were hit on their heads with large rocks. Biz's warning caused Mary to move just enough that the rock hit with only a glancing blow but it was enough to cause her to loose consciousness. The blow to X'akara was much more severe but she was constructed of extremely durable material and it caused no damage. Unfortunately the second blow landed on the access panel in X'akara's neck and pushed the metal in enough to depress the button to deactivate her. She slumped to the ground. Though the creatures tried to grab him and thew rocks at him Biz was able to escape and watched in horror as Mary and X'akara were bound and dragged away.

Chapter 20

The transition from hypervelocity went smoothly and Voltrod turned to his servant CAMCIA and said, “Voltees find L’abart and have him come here immediately. I don’t care if he is still recovering from the transition. I don’t have time for his weakness.”

Voltees connected with the communication module and signaled L’abart’s compartment.

“Sir, there is no answer from L’abart’s compartment. I have sent a messenger to check on him,” Voltees reported to the commander.

“Very well, Voltees. Tell the messenger to drag that disgusting weakling here no matter how much he protests. I am impatient to get on with the search for that child. We have wasted too much time as it is.”

Voltrod fumed and complained until the messenger returned practically dragging a very ill L’abart into the compartment.

“Ah, L’abart,” Voltrod said with a sarcastic grin, “I see you have survived transition once more.”

L’abart attempted to straighten up and glared at Voltrod. “I have indeed survived in spite of the lack of medication which your inferior medication machine failed to dispense prior to transition. This entire ship is a foul smelling, malfunctioning, disorganized, garbage dump and…”

"Enough, you sniveling weakling" roared Voltrod, "If you don't like this ship I will gladly remove you from it along with the rest of the rubbish!"

"Yes," L'abart answered smugly, "You would like to get rid of me but then how would you find the child?"

"Don't tempt me L'abart. You haven't been much use lately and my patience grows thin. Where is she?"

"I sense that she is very far away," L'abart said as he moved slowly and painfully to the three-dimensional star map projected above the navigational console. "I cannot be more specific at this distance but she is somewhere in this system."

Voltrod leaned closer to the display and exclaimed, "That's the Syamin System! Are you sure?"

"Yes she is there," L'abart answered with annoyance, "I am positive as she is no longer traveling. At this distance I can not pinpoint her location but she is probably on one of these planets."

"You better be right, L'abart, though I cannot understand why anyone would travel to that system on purpose. It is known to harbor bandits and pirates who prey on unsuspecting travelers who accidentally wander into that sector. Navigator, plot a course to the Syamin system."

While Voltrod was interviewing L'abart Voltees (X'orige) was checking the medication system. Apparently someone had shut it down prior to transition. He checked the circuits and traced the action back to Amden the maintenance technician.

"I wonder if he is the one causing the other problems with this ship?" Voltees thought. "I think I will give this person a visit. Perhaps we can work together."

"Commander Voltrod," Voltees said soon after transition was completed, "I have detected an error in one of my circuits. With your permission I will have a maintenance tech perform a diagnostic scan to detect and correct the error."

"Yes, by all means. Go immediately to the maintenance compartment and have Amden check it. Do not let anyone else touch your circuits," Voltrod commanded.

Voltees bowed his head to the commander and said, "As you wish," and thought to himself, "Exactly the one I wanted."

When Amden finished the diagnostic scan on Voltees and no error was indicated he was puzzled. "Just exactly what was the error you detected?"

"There was no error," Voltees answered.

"Then why are you here?"

"I ran a check on the medication system after L'abart complained that he was unable to obtain his transition drug. The system had been modified and I was able to trace the path back to your station."

Amden felt as if all the air was knocked out of his lungs and collapsed on a stool as the color drained from his face. "Well I guess I am a dead man," he said resigned to his fate.

"Not necessarily. I didn't tell the commander that you were responsible for the malfunction. I told him is was a moisture leak in the control module."

"It doesn't matter," Amden said with a sigh, "He will know now. The Senior Maintenance Officer put a surveillance monitor in this compartment shortly after I was freed. Apparently he doesn't trust me. It's recording everything you just said."

"No, Amden, our conversation has not been recorded. You are not the only one who can alter circuits on this ship. Your surveillance monitor is currently recording an empty compartment. After we complete our plan I will reactivate the camera and we will record you running a diagnostic scan on me. You will then 'fix' my circuit error. The commander will be relieved that his best maintenance technician was able to repair me. Who knows he may even promote you again."

Amden stared open-mouthed at the CAMCIA. Finally he managed to say, “What plan?”

“Our coordinated plan for the sabotage of this ship. We have both been causing small malfunctions in the ship’s systems that have only resulted in minor problems. Some of our malfunctions have canceled the other one out, such as the medication malfunction. You see I had programmed the machine to dispense a drug that would amplify the effects of transition. You disabled the machine and L’abart was unable to take the medication. But now we can coordinate our efforts and cause much more damage.”

This was the most unbelievable conversation Amden has ever had with a CAMCIA. How could this machine be doing these things, making plans to destroy the ship and most unbelievably lying to the commander?

“What are you?” Amden said shaking his head, “A CAMCIA can not lie?”

“I am a CAMCIA but I was given a unique program that allows me to function independently and fabricate as necessary. I was designed to protect and guard the Sovereign Heir Apparent L’demi.”

“You mean the child the commander has been trying to capture?” Amden asked with astonishment.

“Yes, that child.” Voltees answered.

"But, how did you get on board this ship?" Amden asked and then it dawned on him, "You slipped in with the damaged soldier CAMCIA. Now it all makes sense! I will help you. I might be able to persuade others to join us. There are many unhappy slaves on this ship."

Chapter 21

Mary slowly regained consciousness and found that she was lying face down in the sand with her hands tied behind her. Her head was throbbing with pain and there was sand in her mouth. She tried to sit up but was unable to because her bound feet were drawn up behind her and a rope connected them to her hands. She turned her head and was able to see X'akara was lying close by bound in a similar manner. She called out to her but realized that the CAMCIA must have been deactivated. Biz heard Mary's cry and left his post in the tree to comfort Mary.

"Oh Biz," she whispered as he nuzzled her neck, "what happened?"

Biz chirped with relief to see Mary awake and then signaled to Mary to follow as he flew up into the tree. It was several minutes before Mary realized what he wanted her to do.

"My head hurts so that I don't know if I can do it Biz," she said trying to concentrate. But soon she began to float upward. Mary landed awkwardly on a large branch of the tree and tried to catch her breath. Her escape came none too soon because seconds later one of the creatures that captured her came into view.

The creature appeared to be egg-shaped at the bottom with a smaller rectangular bump above from which a large appendage reached out. At the end of the appendage there was a pincer like hand with a single multifaceted eye extending out on a stalk just above the hand. It was a greasy appearing creature and was a mottled brown and green color with shiny speckles scattered all over. The creature moved smoothly over the ground leaving a slimy gray substance behind it.

Ugh, she thought, *It looks like a slimy rock!*

The creature searched the area for his captive and appeared increasingly agitated when it could find no trace of Mary. It slid away in the direction from which it came with surprising speed.

Mary stared with morbid fascination at the creature as it moved out of site. Biz flew up from his branch and anxiously motioned for her to follow him.

"I guess you are right. We better get away from here before that thing comes back."

Mary's head was throbbing painfully and it took all her concentration to make it back to the cave. When she got there she collapsed onto the floor, totally exhausted but Biz would not let her rest. He dragged a knife to her and helped her use it to cut the bonds that tied her hands. She groaned with relief as the circulation returned to her hands and she gently rubbed the raw and torn skin of her wrists. She washed the sand from her mouth and her face and winced as the water caused the scratches on her face to burn. She reached up and touched the very tender spot on her head where she had been hit. There didn't seem to be any broken skin or bleeding but her head still ached.

"I think I will be alright," she told Biz, "But my head hurts so bad I can't think straight."

Biz disappeared for a moment and returned with a small blue flower. He motioned for Mary to eat one of the tiny pedals. The taste was bitter but within seconds her headache subsided.

"Thanks Biz. I feel much better. Now we need to go and free X'akara before that slimy rock creature does something horrible to her."

Biz insisted that they fly back to X'akara. Mary was barely able to keep up with him and couldn't help but wonder how he could find his way through the thick fog. She suddenly realized just how much she had come to depend on him since they had been on this planet.

"I don't know how you do it," she whispered as he lead her straight back to the place where X'akara lay. "I need to flip her over to get to the door to her control panel," Mary said as she concentrated on moving the CAMCIA. "There I see it. It seems to be jammed closed. I will have to go down there and try to open it manually. Keep a watch out for me please Biz."

Mary floated quietly down to the CAMCIA and was able to slowly pull the damaged door open and push the activation switch. While X'akara's systems rebooted Mary used the knife to cut the bindings. Soon the reboot was complete and X'akara sat up.

"My control panel is open," she said as she reached up to close it. The dented cover depressed the activation button and X'akara slumped to the ground once more.

"Oh no!" Mary shouted too late. "I need to keep her from closing that panel. I know I'll use this rope to tie her hands together. Maybe it will hold until I can tell her not to close the panel."

Mary pushed the activation button. As X'akara's systems booted up she tried to move her arm to close the access panel.

"Don't close the panel door! It is broken." Mary said. "Hurry follow me before they come back."

X'akara easily snapped the rope holding her hands and followed Mary back to the cave where Mary removed the panel door. X'akara used a hammer to straightened it before Mary reinstalled it.

Mary spent an uneasy night worried that the rock creatures would find their cave but Biz seemed to be totally unconcerned.

"How can you be so calm?" she asked Biz, "Do you know something we don't?"

The next morning X'akara scouted the area at the base of the cave and found no evidence of the rock creatures.

"I think we may have stumbled into what they consider to be their territory. If that is so then all we have to do is stay away from that area."

Biz who had been sitting quietly on Mary's shoulder bounced up and down and chirped excitedly.

"I think Biz agrees with you," Mary said with a grin.

X'akara studied the barda's action and said, "Yes, it appears as though he does. I have been watching him and it appears that he possesses a great deal of information about this place. Perhaps we should let him guide us."

Biz puffed up with pride strutted about the cave chirping. Mary couldn't help but laugh at his antics.

"Biz, you are so silly," she said giggling.

X'akara, who despite her attempts at becoming more relaxed, didn't see the humor.

"We won't get anything done if you are too busy acting foolish," she said sternly to Biz as she prepared to go out in search of food and water for Mary.

Biz stopped in mid step and flew to Mary for protection. Mary snuggled the little barda close and said, "Don't worry Biz, X'akara is not mad at you. She doesn't understand that you can have fun and get something accomplished too. She won't hurt you. Will you, X'akara!"

"Of course not," X'akara answered.

They continued their exploration of the planet being careful not to go into the rock creatures' territory. With Biz's help they found many edible plants to supplement their stores. Biz also found a small waterfall not far from the cave. At the bottom of the waterfall was a small pool that was just right for swimming.

Mary, who had never learned to swim, found she had a natural aptitude and quickly learned to swim and dive in the cool water. Biz would sit at the water's edge daintily splashing water over his body and grooming his feathers but would never go out any further.

X'akara would have nothing to do with the water even though her covering was watertight. Her interest in the pool lay in catching the aquatic animals that inhabited the pool. She found several different species and had Biz to inspect each one. He checked out each one and chirped with approval on all but one. On that one he grasped his throat and pretended to gag and fall over in a dead faint.

"You don't have to be so dramatic," X'akara said tersely, "A simple negative shake of the head would suffice."

But though she didn't appreciate his acting she did trust his judgement and quickly threw the animal back into the water.

As the days passed Mary became accustomed to the fog and even learned to find her way about with more confidence. Finding food was becoming easier as well and there was more time for relaxation. Mary was almost enjoying herself in spite of her surrounding but she did miss the sun.

X'akara was not faring as well as Mary and Biz. The constant moisture was seeping into her systems in spite of her watertight skin and she was concerned about her power supply. Normally on the ship she could recharge on a regular basis. When she was on the surface of a planet she would recharge with solar power but the dense fog on this planet kept out the rays of the sun.

She began conserving power as much as possible but she knew that it was only a matter of time until she ran out of power. Because of this she pushed Mary to quickly learn as much as possible about the planet but didn't share the reason with her.

Mary noticed that X'akara was slowing down during the day and shutting down completely at night. It didn't take her long to figure out that there was a problem. She finally asked, "X'akara, what can I do to help you? I know you are losing power."

"There is nothing you can do. I had planned to tell you soon but since you are aware of my loss of power, I see no reason to continue. I am going to shut down completely to conserve what power I have left for an emergency. You are capable of caring for yourself. You know your way around and what foods to eat. You will be fine without me."

X'akara went to the back of the cave and prepared for shut down. She gave Mary a few last instructions before Mary pressed the deactivation button on X'akara's control panel. Mary wrapped the CAMCIA in an oil-soaked blanket and slowly walked to the front of the cave. Tears streamed down her face as she looked out at the fog the enveloped the land. Biz landed on Mary's shoulder and comforted her.

"Biz, I know she is just a machine but I feel so sad. I hate this fog! I wish we had never come here!"

Biz could only coo and snuggle close. There was nothing he could do to ease her pain except be there and listen to her sobbing. She cried herself to sleep holding the tiny barda close.

She awoke the next morning with her eyes burning from all her tears and a determination to search for a power source. With a heavy heart she floated down to the ground. She missed X'akara's constant scolding to use rope and pulley to descend. She began the daily search for food.

She didn't feel much like eating but she knew she needed to keep her strength up.

"Somehow I will find a way to get power for X'akara," she shouted. "I will find a way!"

Mary had been trained very well and she was able to obtain and cook her daily food without much trouble. She never had to worry about getting lost because Biz was always able to find their way home. Soon she settled in a routine and was happy at times. She kept a close check on X'akara, making sure the oil blanket was in place and moisture was kept away from her. A fire in the cave helped keep it dry, although it was a little too warm at times. When she had stockpiled a supply of food she began to explore further away from the cave. She relied on Biz to keep her from harm, still wondering how he knew so much about the planet.

One day when they had wondered far from the cave they came upon an area totally different from the terrain they had previously explored. The plants here were enormous, as big around as large trees, stretching up out of sight in the fog. At first there were just a few large plants but as they traveled further into the area they came to a forest of the plants. The plants were larger and closer together and inside the forest it was dark and foreboding. Mary turned to go back to the cave but Biz wanted to go into the forest.

"Surely you don't want me to go in there!" Mary said. "It looks scary to me."

But Biz showed no fear and flew straight into the darkness under the towering plants.

"Oh well, if you think it is safe, I will go, but I don't like it at all," Mary said as she walked into the forest.

When her eyes adjusted to the darkness she found she could see better than she had imagined, but not well enough to feel comfortable. She would have turned back but Biz kept urging her on.

"Biz, you better have a good reason for going into this scary place. I don't like it at all."

Biz chirped happily and continued deeper into the forest. He seemed so excited and happy that Mary couldn't help but start to lose some of her fear. They kept traveling for a long time and Mary was concerned about getting back to the cave before night.

"Biz, we have to go back now. We will barely get back to the cave before dark as it is," she said as Biz continued on through the forest. "Biz, come back," she shouted anxiously as he disappeared in the darkness. "Please don't leave me!"

She lost track of time as she waited for Biz to return. It seemed like a very long time and she was afraid to move. She sat down on the forest floor completely exhausted and very scared. "Oh please come back," she cried, but there was no answer.

She had no way of knowing how long she sat there completely miserable when she noticed a tiny light flickering above her. It moved about the forest twinkling in the darkness. "It must be a small insect," she thought remembering the fireflies she used to see on a summer's night on earth. The diversion of watching the small creature flitting about helped to calm her and she was disappointed when it flew away and a deep loneliness settled over her.

"I can't believe Biz deserted me!" she said as the tears began to fall, "Why doesn't he come back. I need him so. Why doesn't he love me anymore."

Mary lay down on the forest floor and rested her head on her arm, the tears soaking her sleeve. She had never felt so lost and alone, not even on Earth when she thought no one loved her. She had felt Biz's love and now felt betrayed. It was more than she could bear.

Eventually Mary fell into a fitful sleep. In her dream she was trying to run from some unseen menace but she couldn't move. She tried to scream but no sound came out. She awoke with a start and sat up trembling with her heart pounding. The forest was much darker now and Mary was cold and hungry.

“How,” she said, “am I going to find my way home? Oh, Biz please come back!” The reality of her situation was worse that the nightmare.

Suddenly thousands of tiny lighted creatures descended from above and surrounded Mary. Some of the creatures flew in closer and touched her hands and her face. Others hovered over her head and examined individual strands of her hair. They didn’t make a sound except for a faint tinkle that almost sounded like laughter. They resembled tiny stands of very bright light wound loosely into a ball with some strands gracefully floating below and behind as they flew around her. When they brushed against her skin it felt like a puff of warm tingly air.

Mary felt that they meant her no harm and she tried to relax and concentrate on picking up their thoughts. One of the tiny creatures seemed to understand what Mary was attempting and flew in very close to Mary stopping inches from her face. Suddenly Mary felt wave of peaceful happiness flood her brain with so much force that she toppled over backward.

“Wow! You might be tiny but you sure are powerful!” Mary said to the tiny being floating above her as she slowly sat up. The ball of light dipped slightly as if to acknowledge Mary’s words and with a tinkle rose higher above Mary. The others gathered around it and they slowly moved away. Somehow Mary knew they wanted her to follow them.

They had traveled through the dark foggy forest for what seemed like a very long time and as Mary tired she wondered how much further they would go. She was also worried that Biz, if he ever came back, wouldn't be able to find her.

Lost in her thoughts Mary didn't see the glow in the distance at first. Then she felt the rising excitement of the group of tiny beings and was amazed at the sight in the distance. There in the gloomy forest was a huge domed crystal structure glowing from within and sparkling in a multitude of colors magically lighting up the forest. As they moved closer Mary realized that it was much larger than she had first imagined. She leaned back as far as she could but could not see all the way to the top.

"This is the most beautiful place I have ever seen!" she said rising upward with the group to the entry located high on the outer wall. Mary paused in the entrance completely awed by the spectacle below her.

"Wow, this is even more amazing that the outside. It's a city of crystal buildings inside a crystal dome. How wonderful," she said floating with the group toward the largest building in the center of the city. The whole place glowed with warm and comforting light and the tinkle of the tiny creatures filled the air.

When they reached the building they paused outside large ornate crystal doors that were guarded by two of the lighted beings that were much larger and more subdued in their colors. After a moment the doors opened and they were ushered into a long chamber. At the far end of the room resting on a raised platform was a being similar to the ones escorting Mary, but much larger and brighter. Mary could feel the power emanating from it even from the end of the long chamber. The group became very subdued and quiet. She knew she was in the presence of a great and powerful leader.

Mary felt rather than heard the leader ask the group to leave. She turned to go with the others but paused as she heard the leader speak in a voice that sounded a like the tinkling of bells. She could clearly understand the words.

"Mary Smith, please stay."

Mary turned around and moved slowly toward the leader. When she stood in front of the leader she bowed her head and tried to think of something to say. *What do you say to royalty,* she thought.

"Well, it has been my experience that the first thing you should say to royalty is Hello your Highness," the leader said with a tinkling laugh, "So I will begin by saying 'Hello your Highness'."

"Well, I guess I should also say Hello, your Highness," Mary said with a bow.

"Oh you must not call me your Highness," the leader said, "I am not royalty. I am Abarab the Aeroleet Defender, chosen to lead and protect the

Aeroleet. A powerful position to be sure, but not royalty. But you, my friend, if I may be so bold as to call you friend, are indeed royalty."

Mary was again at a loss for words but managed to say, "Hello Abarab Aeroleet Defender." She smiled at Abarab and then thought *how did you know I was royalty? I didn't even know until recently.*

"We Aeroleet know the legend of The Sovereign Heir Apparent L'demi. The one whose birth was kept a secret from the evil ones and how she was taken to a secret place far, far away from Ayri so she would be kept safe until she could grow powerful enough to return and defeat the evil Bahadin. I am honored to be in your presence."

Mary was overwhelmed by Abarab's words and said, "I am afraid you will be disappointed by me. I am not what you think I am."

"Oh, no, you are everything I have heard and more. You have the potential and the power. I feel it very strongly. All you lack is the confidence and you will gain that in time. But now I feel you are very tired and hungry and I am ashamed to have kept your standing there so long. Come, we will go to my private chambers and we will talk while you rest and have nourishment." Abarab said as she spread her wings and flew ahead to lead Mary though a door and down a hall to her private chambers, "You must tell me all the details of your travels and how you came to be known as Mary Smith."

While Mary was eating she told Abarab of her life on Earth and her travels so far. She hesitated at telling about New Quain.

Abarab interrupted saying, "Oh the underground world. We have known about that for a long time. Can't say as I blame them. Their old planet Quain was almost completely destroyed by the Bahadin. Nothing left there but a few plants in remote areas and that disgusting mining operation they built with slave labor. You must believe me when I tell you your secrets are safe with me."

"I believe you." Mary said, "I don't know why, but I do."

Abarab glowed a little brighter and her voice tinkled with joy when she said, "You honor me with your trust. I will not betray you secrets. But now, I can see you are very tired. I will leave you to rest. I look forward to continuing our conversation. Perhaps you would like a tour of the city later."

Mary, who was indeed very tired, fought the desire to sleep and said, "I can't stay. I have to get back to the forest."

"But why do you wish to leave us? Have I offended you?"

"No, Abarab, you have been very kind, but I must go back. Biz, my little barda left me there. If he comes back and I am gone he will be worried."

"Oh my!" Mary exclaimed as she jumped up to leave, "What if he has already come back. He won't know where I am. I really have to go. I don't think I can stand it if I lose him!"

"Mary, I am so sorry! I forgot to tell you!" Abarab said apologetically as she motioned for Mary to sit down, "Your Biz knows you are here. He met one of our sentinels in the forest and told her that you were too tired and hungry to continue on with him and he asked her if she would lead you to our city and watch over you until he returns. She had a difficult time finding you and then was uncertain how to communicate with you when she did find you. She came back here to get help. It took much longer than it should have. I know Biz would be upset if he knew how long you waited, alone. He was sorry to have to leave you but he was excited about finding his family."

"Family?" Mary asked, "How can that be? He is from New Quain."

"That is a long story," Abarab said settling down beside Mary, "It began when some of the Syamin Pirates decided that attacking space ships was getting a little too dangerous. They looked around for an easier way to make a living. The pirates had noticed that some travelers, especially humanoids, often had small pets that accompanied them on their journeys. They searched the planets near by and when they came across the barda they thought they had found the perfect pets. The barda were small and cheerful and easy to feed. The pirates sat about capturing the trusting and gentle barda and placed them in cages. They traveled about the other solar systems where they were unknown and tried to sell the barda but their plans didn't turn out as they expected.

The pirates were lazy and didn't give the kind of care the barda needed to survive. They forgot to give the barda food and water on a regular basis, which caused them to weaken and become sick. But the worst thing the pirates did was to lock the barda in individual cages. Denied the contact with other living creatures some of the barda gave up hope and died. When the pirates reached the market they were only able to sell a few barda and the ones they sold were returned. A barda only makes a good companion when a special bond is formed between the barda and its humanoid.

With most of the barda sick and dying the pirates decided selling barda wasn't such a good idea and dumped the remaining barda on several planets including New Quain and returned home.

The barda, released from captivity thrived. Little did the pirates know that they were partially right about the barda. They could become wonderful companions for humanoids, forming life long bonds, but only when both the barda and the humanoids were free to chose."

Mary sat down on the soft pallet and took a sip of water. "So Biz was one of the barda that was captured?" she asked.

"Oh yes," Abarab answered, "he was very young when he was taken away and his family grieved for him. I know they will be overjoyed to see him."

"Do you think he will really come back to me?" Mary asked almost afraid to hear the answer.

"Mary, don't worry. Biz would never desert you. I can feel the strong bond that flows between you two. Now try not to worry and get some rest. He will be back."

Mary lay down on the soft bed that had been made ready for her and thought about all the things she had learned. Soon she fell asleep with the soft musical tinkling of the Aeroleet voices soothing her.

Mary awoke slowly, stretching in the wonderfully soft bed. When she heard Biz's soft chirp her eyes flew open and she exclaimed with joy, "Oh Biz! You are back! I'm so glad to see you. I missed you so much."

Biz snuggled close to Mary's neck and chirped cheerfully. "I should have known you would never leave me," she said as she petted her beloved Biz.

She was so caught up in the joy of welcoming Biz that it was a few minutes before she noticed the quiet group of barda that surrounded her bed. "Oh my, Biz," she exclaimed, "Is this your family? They are so beautiful!"

The barda that surrounded her were indeed beautiful, their feathers shinning in a multitude of colors. There were small barda and large barda and all sizes in-between. One large barda, with deep rich burgundy feathers and an air of authority, stared solemnly at Mary while the others watched in anticipation. He flew close to Mary's face and gazed intensely into her eyes. Immediately Mary felt his power wash over her and sat helplessly as his mind explored the deepest parts of her very being. Suddenly he let out a loud chirp of approval and Mary was engulfed in waves of happiness as the entire group swarmed around her chirping joyfully.

"I am pleased that I have passed your examination," she said a little shakily to the dignified barda that still hovered in front of her, "I will cherish the honor of being approved as a companion for Biz."

Biz, his eyes shining with joy, snuggled close to Mary's neck and cooed softly. He always knew that Mary was the only companion for him, but it was comforting to have his Elder's approval as was proper for his kind. As he rested on Mary's shoulder he thought about the joyous reunion with his family and how happy they were to see him.

The only sad part was confirming that some of his fellow captives had not survived their harsh treatment at the hands of the pirates.

Biz's parents were pleased to see him and happy that he had a companion but they insisted that the Elder approve the companion. So it was that they all traveled to see if Mary would meet with approval.

The Aeroleet, who had been waiting politely until the Elder had finished, joined in the joyous celebration. They brought out food and filled the air with their twinkling lights and happy voices.

If I can never leave here to find my own family, she thought, *at least I can enjoy Biz's family and my good friends the Aeroleet.*

Chapter 22

While Mary was celebrating with the Aeroleet and Biz's family the Bahadin Warship Falconoid was traveling to the Syamin Galaxy at hypervelocity. *Soon,* thought Commander Voltrod, *I will capture that child. She will not escape me this time!* His face screwed up in a smile that appeared more repulsive than his usual frown as he thought of the honors and promotions he would receive when the high command heard of his accomplishment. He could almost hear the roar of the crowd on his home planet as the ruler announced that he, Voltrod, had single handedly brought about the defeat of Ayri. Voltrod had no way of knowing that his dream of glory was about to turn into a nightmare.

Amden and Voltees working together had formed a network of slaves and reprogrammed CAMCIA. Much of the ship's monitoring systems had been altered giving the revolutionaries safe areas in which to meet and plan their next moves. They were performing sabotage throughout the ship making life miserable for the Bahadin. Garbage recycling units clogged and overflowed into the compartments of the Bahadin. Food dispensers malfunctioned and a foul odor filled the air throughout the ship.

A mild poison was injected into the food of the Bahadin and they became sick and were sent to the infirmary. The physician, who was a slave captured on Pouder, made sure the sick Bahadin were unable to return to work because the medicine he gave them was the same poison that had made them sick.

When Voltrod complained that his crew was not improving the physician told the Commander that he had isolated the cause as a new strain of virus that is highly contagious and resistant to all the medications he had in the infirmary.

"They will just have to tough it out, sir, until the virus has run its course. There is no cure for it," the physician informed the commander.

"If that is so," Voltrod shouted, "Why are the slaves not affected?"

The physician bowed his head, barely able to contain his composure, and said, "It is my humble opinion that myself and the other slaves, being a different species, have a natural immunity to the virus. I suggest that you limit your contact with the infected men. But now, Commander, I humbly beg you to allow me to return to the infirmary so that I may attend my patients."

"Very well, go," Voltrod said gruffly.

When the physician had exited the compartment Commander Voltrod turned to Voltees and asked, "What is your assessment of the physician's report?"

"Sir, I have monitored his findings and believe he is correct," Voltees answered.

The physician exited the compartment and headed back to the infirmary. He encountered Amden in the passageway and pulled him into a safe area where he began to laugh uncontrollably.

"Physician, control yourself," Amden said shaking the physician, "What is so funny?"

The physician took a deep breath, and began to tell Amden what he had told the Commander. "The look on his face when I told him the slaves were immune was priceless. I almost laughed in his face. I thought he was going to explode. He will probably have Voltees spraying disinfectant all over the command compartment."

Amden patted the physician on the back and said, "Well done my friend. Be careful though. The Commander isn't stupid."

"Oh, I intend to stay as far from him as possible. Keep me informed on the next step. I have to get back now to treat those poor sick Bahadin," the physician said with a smirk as he left the safe area.

Within weeks the ship was almost entirely run by slaves and the reprogrammed CAMCIA as more and more Bahadin became too sick to work.

The most dangerous threat to the plan to take over the ship was L'abart with his power to read others thoughts. Fortunately, L'abart shielded his mind from the slaves, believing their thoughts far too unintelligent and insignificant to monitor. Just to be on the safe side Voltees added a powerful tranquilizer to L'abart's food keeping him asleep much of the time and groggy and disoriented when he was awake.

Voltees and Amden decided to wait until after they reached the Syamin Galaxy and L'abart had given his traitorous information about Mary's location to Voltrod before they took over the ship.

Everything was ready for the mutiny when the warship transitioned into normal space. L'abart's tranquilizer had worn off by the time Voltrod summoned him to the command compartment.

L'abart entered the compartment with a swagger, feeling more alert than he had in quite a while swelled with his own self-importance and superiority.

Voltrod ignored him as long as possible and then with a sneer said, "I see you managed to survive transition this time, but enough of this small talk. Where is the child?"

L'abart managed to retain his composure as he smiled at Voltrod. *Just you wait,* he thought, *As soon as you kill that child, I will personally get rid of you. Not quickly but slowly and painfully.*

He walked over to the star chart and paused for a moment pretending to concentrate. Then with a flourish he pointed to a planet and said, "She is here on Netula."

"Are you sure?" Voltrod asked.

"Of course I am sure! How could you doubt me?" L'abart answered with disdain.

"Very well then," Voltrod said as he brushed his whiskers with his paw. The guard standing behind L'abart saw the signal from Voltrod and pushed a needle against L'abart's neck and injected the poison.

L'abart never knew what hit him.

"Get that garbage out of my sight," Voltrod commanded as he turned to his navigator, "Plot a course to Netula."

The navigator glanced at Voltees who with a nod of his head indicated that he should proceed. The planned take over of the ship was being carried out systematically throughout the vessel as they turned toward Netula. Voltrod and his personal guards were the last Bahadin to be captured.

Chapter 23

L'Alie, Sovereign Ruler of Ayri, paced the floor of the royal residence at Merald, the capital city of Ayri. She was worried about her youngest son. The latest attack by the Bahadin had begun shortly after L'amie had gone to the city with his Drillmaster. The Bahadin had been pounding the planet with such a large number of missiles that the force shield was beginning to deteriorate. It was only a matter of time until they would be able to penetrate the shield.

L'amie felt his Mother's anxiety and silently communicated his reassurance that he was on his way home. He then closed his mind to hide his concern that he probably would not make it back before the shield collapsed. On his own he would have been able to move quickly but his Drillmaster held him up.

The Drillmaster was tall and thin and walked with a pronounced limp, the result of many injuries received over the years as self defense instructor to the royal children. L'amie thought he was ancient and indeed he had served many generations. His face was long and narrow and was lined with many wrinkles. The top of his head was bald with a fringe of short gray hair covering the sides.

"Go on L'amie, do not wait for me," the Drillmaster said pausing to catch his breath, "You mother needs you."

L'amie ignored the Drillmaster's request and waited patiently for him to catch his breath. He tried to remember the location of the nearest shelter while his teacher leaned against the wall of the clothier's shop.

"Isn't there a shelter near here?" L'amie asked the Drillmaster.

"Yes, L'amie, it is just around the corner but it is not as secure as the shelter at the royal residence. If you hurry you can still make it home. Leave me here. I will go to this shelter as soon as I rest a minute."

"I will not leave you," L'amie said stubbornly, as he moved to the side of the frail Drillmaster. "Just lean on me and we will soon be in the shelter."

They moved slowly down the street, the Drillmaster leaning heavily on his young student. They had almost made it to the shelter when the first missile penetrated the shield and exploded behind them. The force of the explosion knocked them down severely injuring the Drillmaster's leg.

L'amie shook off the debris that covered him and said, "Drillmaster, can you get up? We must get to the shelter before another missile hits."

"L'amie, I can not. I fear that my leg is broken. Please leave me and go to the shelter," the Drillmaster pleaded.

But L'amie would not leave his beloved Drillmaster to die in the street. He bound the injured leg as best he could with strips torn from his shirt. Then he pulled the Drillmaster towards the shelter. He was near exhaustion when some of the people in the shelter felt his silent call for help and rushed to help pull the Drillmaster into the shelter.

"Thank you L'amie," the Drillmaster said as the rescuers pulled him into the shelter, "You are truly a wonderful and brave boy."

It was the last thing L'amie ever heard. L'amie was just inside the door when the next missile hit destroying the entrance and instantly killing L'amie, Mary's twin brother.

In the palace his mother collapsed as a wave of sorrow engulfed the entire planet. Every individual on Ayri felt the loss of L'amie and the grief of his family.

Far away on Netula as Mary was celebrating her reunion with Biz, when a sudden wrenching pain engulfed her. She felt as if her entire body was being torn apart and she screamed as she collapsed in a dead faint. Biz, alarmed by the intense emotions radiating from Mary, landed close by her neck and attempted to comfort her but Mary didn't awake from her faint. Biz's family hovered close by her side comforting Biz and trying to comfort Mary. The Aeroleet also felt the powerful emotion and gathered around her.

Abarab closely examined Mary and when she had finished she said, "Biz, Mary has had a great shock. Her body still lives but her spirit has flown far away. You must concentrate all your powers together with us to bring her spirit back as soon as possible. The longer her spirit is away from her body the harder it will be for it to find its way back."

So Biz's family and the Aeroleet joined together to pull Mary's spirit back.

Mary felt herself drawn through a great darkness toward a tiny speck of light that she somehow knew was waiting for her. Though she felt that she traveled a very long way it only took a few seconds. As she grew near the speck of light took the shape of a young boy and she instantly she knew it was her twin. A flood of happiness surrounded her as she embraced her brother.

"My twin, my brother!" she exclaimed, "I have never seen you but I feel as if I have always known you. What is this place?"

"This is the space the spirit travels between the living world and the place we go when we die," L'amie answered.

"Are we dead?" Mary asked.

"I am, but you are not."

"But I am here with you. Doesn't that mean I am dead too?"

"No, you are still alive. We have been allowed to meet here so I can give you a message. I wish we could have met in life, but it was not meant to be. I have always felt your presence because you are a part of me."

"But, L'amie we are together now."

"Yes, but only for a short time. You must return and I must go on to the light," L'amie said pointing to the beautiful tunnel of light glowing in the darkness.

"Can't I go with you?" Mary asked hypnotized by the peaceful joy that flowed from the tunnel entrance.

"No, not now. You must return, as your work is not finished," L'amie said and turned Mary to face away from the light as he continued, "Please listen carefully and remember what I say. Tell our parents that I love them and I am sad to leave them but I have fulfilled my destiny and I go on to a better place."

"What is the message you have been given for me?" Mary asked.

"Always trust in your deepest feelings and never let evil into your heart. I am to tell you that you will be the most powerful Sovereign ever to reign Ayri and you will lead our people to victory over the Bahadin and free the Bahadin race from the bondage of their corrupt rulers."

Mary turned and gazed deep into her brother's eyes and knew in her heart that what he said was true but she didn't feel like a powerful ruler. "How can I do all these things?" she cried.

"It will happen," L'amie said as he embraced Mary once again and turned to leave, "Now it is time for you to go back. Be brave and remember what I said."

Mary watched as the spirit of her twin glided into the tunnel and was engulfed in the beautiful light. And then the tunnel was gone and she was completely surrounded by darkness. She was very afraid and realized that she didn't know how to get back. The darkness seemed to thicken and she was smothered by her fear and she panicked.

"How can I get back?" she screamed as she started to cry.

Suddenly in the midst of her terror she felt a calmness flow over her and a beautiful peaceful voice said, "Be still and you will be guided by the love of your friends."

Mary let go of her fear and concentrated. Then from far, far away she felt a pull like a tiny thread attached to her heart. It was the thoughts of Biz and the Aeroleet guiding her back to her body.

The spark of life in Mary's body had grown very small. It had been so long since her collapse that some of the barda had given up hope, but Biz remained determined to save her. The Aeroleet hovered near Mary. They never doubted Mary would return. Biz was not surprised, but he was very happy and relieved when Mary's eyes flickered and then opened. Biz's loud and long chirp brought joy to the group surrounding Mary's bed.

When Abarab examined Mary she announced with joy, "Mary's spirit has returned. She will recover!"

Biz flew in circles above her bed chirping joyously celebrating her spirit's return. Then exhausted by the excitement and the anxiety he had endured he snuggled close to Mary and promptly went to sleep.

In the days that followed Mary told Biz and Abarab of her journey and the things her brother had told her. Mary was very weak and depressed and couldn't seem to shake the feeling of loss. Biz stayed close and comforted her but it was Abarab who to put into words the things Mary needed to hear to begin healing.

Mary was weeping when she said, "Abarab, I know this sounds crazy because I never met my brother and I didn't really know him but I feel like part of me is missing that can never be replaced. It makes me so sad."

"Somewhere in your subconscious mind you were always aware of him even though you didn't know it," Abarab said wisely, "You will always feel the loss of your brother, but in time the pain will ease. You were given a wonderful gift to be able to visit his spirit before he left this universe. Hold that memory close and it will comfort you."

Chapter 24

The space ship Esmera from New Quain was attacked by the Syamin pirates only minutes after it transitioned from hypervelocity. The battle was fierce but the Esmera was managing to hold the attackers at bay. Esmera's Captain, Arman shouted orders to the crew as more pirate ships appeared on the screen.

"Keep a sharp look out there are more of them coming from the upper quadrant. Don't let them get a tractor beam on us."

Nolus answered, "Got them covered, Captain. I'm sure glad Granny Mer warned us about the pirates and made us study the defense system and made us practice while we were traveling. We would have been a sitting duck if not for her."

"Well, Nolus," Arman said as another missile exploded on the ship's shields, "We aren't out of this yet."

"I know," Nolus answered, "But I thought they would have given up by now. Granny Mer said they only like easy targets."

Then without warning the Pirates broke off the battle and quickly departed in all directions.

"Well, I guess they had enough of us!" Nolus said swelling with pride, "We were just too tough for that bunch." Nolus turned to Arman with a grin but Arman didn't return his smile.

"Nolus, they weren't running from us. Take a look at what just transitioned behind us," Arman said, the color draining from his face.

A huge Bahadin warship had appeared in space behind the Esmera. It's enormous size dwarfing the Esmera.

"What do we do now?" Nolus said.

"There is nothing we can do," Arman answered. "That thing has enough firepower to crush a 100 ships our size without even using the big guns. I'm surprised it hasn't already done so."

"Captain, I am receiving a message from the Bahadin ship," the Communications Officer said.

"Put it on the speaker," Amden ordered.

"Unidentified ship, this is the Warship Falconoid, please identify yourself and your mission."

Amden pressed the switch on the microphone and answered, "This is the Esmera. We have come to rescue the crew of a shipwreck."

"Esmera, lower your shields and prepare to be towed aboard the Falconoid. Power down your weapons. You will not be harmed."

Arman looked at his crew and ordered, "Do as he says. We don't really have a choice."

As the Esmera was being towed toward the Falconoid Arman thought back to when they began this journey. It seemed only a short time ago that Granny anxiously called Arman to her home.

"Arman, Mary is in trouble," Granny began as soon as Arman entered her kitchen, "I was straightening the kitchen when I was hit with a powerful wave of anxiety. I could almost see Mary crying out for help. We have got to do something."

Granny's face was pale and she griped the edge of the table for support as she sat down and reached for Arman's hand.

Arman knelt beside his beloved Grandmother and comforted her as best he could. "What can we do?" he asked.

"Arman, we must go to her."

"But how can we do that, Granny, we don't know where she is, and even if we did how could be get there? All the ships were dismantled to build the tunnels long ago."

Granny managed a smile and said, "Not all the ships were dismantled. There are two ships hidden in the outermost corridor of the storage sector. One is a transport but the other is a fully armed warship.

"A warship!" Arman exclaimed. "We have never had any warships."

"No, we didn't have any when we escaped from Quain but after the tunnels were completed the Council took parts from several transport ships to make one large warship. Then they converted the tunnel lasers into weapons. They worked in secret for many years to perfect the system."

"But why did they do that? I thought we were safe here." Arman said.

"The Council feared another attack, even though we were hidden. The transport ship would be used to save a few selected citizens if the Bahadin attacked this planet. The warship would be able to protect that ship. That way at least some of our people would survive. Only members of the Council and the ones chosen to escape knew about the ships."

Arman sat beside Granny Mer and shook his head. "How is that going to help us? The Council will never permit us to use the ship, and even in the unlikely event they did, who could fly it?"

"I wasn't going to ask the Council. And you will command the ship."

"Me!" Arman exclaimed, "I know nothing about space ships. I've never even been inside one. What made you think I could possibly command the warship?"

"I will teach you. I was a pretty good pilot in my day. It's not really hard. The ship is completely automated. Why," Granny said with a smile, "With a little help from me you will be able to completely control the ship with ease."

"Granny, I think you have lost your mind," Arman said as he patted Granny's hand.

Granny grasped Arman's hand with both her hands and closed her eyes. Arman felt a shock of electrical current flow up his arm as he tried to pull away. Soon his mind was engulfed in the white-hot flow of knowledge from Granny. The intensity of the connection between them increased until Granny broke the link and Arman collapsed on the floor. He awoke a few minutes later.

"What did you do to me? My head is aching," he said rubbing his eyes and the back of his neck.

"Just a little thought transfer to help you fly the ship," Granny replied with a grin. "Come here and I will give you something for your headache."

"But how did you do that? I thought you could only send thoughts to a willing subject and I certainly wasn't willing."

"As far as I know I am the only left that can transfer knowledge that way. The Council banned its use long ago. But when have I ever followed the rules?" Granny said with a smile.

"I have a feeling that I am going to be in a lot of trouble soon," Arman said with a shrug of resignation. He could never refuse Granny's requests and secretly he was excited at the prospect of flying off to rescue Mary.

It didn't take long to locate the hidden ship and prepare it for the voyage ahead. Granny hand picked the crew, including Nolus, and gave each one the knowledge they needed to handle the ship.

The night they left Granny stood with the young men and watched as the enormous doors to the storage chamber opened to the night sky.

"When we get free of the planet's gravitational pull we will stop long enough for me to get a better fix on Mary's location. I'm glad I gave her that homing device. I think she is on one of the planets in the Syamin system. If that is where she is, then we will have to be prepared when we transition from hypervelocity. That area is notorious for pirates."

"Pirates?" Arman exclaimed anxiously, "You never said there would be pirates. What are you getting us into?"

"Don't worry, Arman. They don't usually attack warships. If we fight back they should give up. They prefer unarmed transports, or at least they did long ago when transports from our home world accidentally strayed into their space. Who knows, they might not be there now."

Arman sighed and shook his head as he remembered the night they left and how excited the crew was when they left New Quain. They thought they would rescue Mary and return home as heroes. He turned to his friend Nolus and said, "I'm sorry I got you into this."

Nolus stood and patted his friend on the back, "Arman, I wouldn't have missed it for the world. We had a great time right up until that warship appeared behind us."

Granny reached the bridge just before the tractor beam brought the Esmera into the Falconoid's hold.

"Don't worry children," she said, "I have a feeling this isn't as bad as it seems."

"What do you mean, Granny? What could be worse? We've been captured by a Bahadin Warship!" Arman shouted and then turned his head away, ashamed that he had yelled at his Grandmother.

He struggled to regain his composure and then, he turned back to her and said, "I'm sorry. I didn't mean it."

"Don't be sorry, Arman. You have every right to be alarmed, but I still have the feeling that they mean us no harm," Granny said with assurance.

"Well I hope you are right," Arman said with a spark of hope beginning to grow inside him. "After all they could've blasted us out of the sky, but they didn't.

When the Esmera was secure in the docking bay and the chamber recompressed and safe to enter, Arman opened the hatch and started out. Granny followed close behind.

"Granny, I think you should stay in our ship with the crew," Arman said trying to protect her.

"No, Arman, I got you into this and I will go with you," Granny insisted with a smile, "I am getting the most unusual thoughts from the inhabitants of this ship. I feel an evil Bahadin presence but the mostly I am feeling waves of happiness. I don't think anyone has ever received a happy feeling from any Bahadin warship."

"I feel it too now, Granny. It's very strange," Arman agreed.

They walked down the ramp and were greeted by a CAMCIA soldier. "Please follow me and I will take you to our commander," he said motioning for Arman and Granny to follow.

"They have artificial gravity!" Arman said helping his unsteady grandmother to walk across the docking bay.

"Yes, I heard that they were more advanced in space travel than we were. What a luxury!" Granny answered as she leaned heavily on Arman. Her body was not as quick to adjust to gravity as her young Grandson's was.

When they reached the Command Center they were amazed to see a young man dressed in slave's clothing and a CAMCIA occupying the Command Chairs.

"Welcome to the Warship Falconoid," he said when they were inside the chamber, "My name is X'orige but I am sometimes called Voltees. This young man," he said motioning to the slave, "is Amden. We are the commanders of this ship."

Granny and Arman looked first at the CAMCIA and the young man dressed in Slave's clothing with amazement.

"I can see from your expressions that you are surprised to see a CAMCIA and a former Slave running a Bahadin warship. We will be happy to tell you how we managed the mutiny and takeover later. But now, I am curious as to why and how you were in the Syamin System in the most unusual battleship I have ever seen. It appears to be a converted transport from Quain."

Arman stepped forward and said, "We are the survivors of Quain."

"That's interesting because the most recent information I had stated that there were no survivors from that planet."

Granny was listening to what the CAMCIA said but also to the thoughts of the men in the Command Center. What she heard convinced her that they were in no danger. She could tell that Arman was also listening to the others thoughts and she knew he agreed with her. She was not surprised when he began to tell the CAMCIA their story.

"We are from New Quain," Arman began, "A few of our people escaped the Bahadin's destruction of our home planet, Quain, and over the many years since that time we have been living underground on New Quain. No one has been able to detect our presence there so far.

Not too long ago a small child landed on our planet in a shuttle. Meteors had damaged the oxygen generators on her ship and she was sent down to the planet alone while the CAMCIA made repairs on the ship. We couldn't let the shuttle or the child stay on the surface because we were afraid the Bahadin would spot them. So we decided to take her down into the tunnels with us and hide her ship. She stayed with us until her CAMCIA completed the repairs. While she was with us we grew to love her and hated to see her leave. Now she is in trouble once again so we have come to rescue her."

X'orige processed this information and then asked, "Who is this child that you would risk your lives to rescue her?"

Arman hesitated for a moment but Granny answered for him, "Her name is Mary Smith."

Granny felt the surprise and shock of the one named Amden and heard his sharp intake of breath. *So I was right"* she thought, *If I could read the thoughts of a CAMCIA I bet his reaction would have been just as strong.*

X'orige was not expecting the answer he heard. He went to the control panel to download information from the captured ship's navigation computer. Then he consulted the latest star charts in the Falconoid's navigation system. "Yes," he said to himself, "the planet from which they traveled would have been near the trajectory taken by Mary's ship from Earth and given the recent passage of a rogue Comet in that area, it is likely that Mary's ship could have encountered meteors." Then he turned to the group of travelers and said, "I believe we are in search of the same child."

It was Arman's turn to be surprised. "What!" he exclaimed.

"It is true," X'orige answered, "The same Mary Smith that you came to rescue is the one that I too have come to help. We have much to discuss and plans to make."

Amden smiled as he said to the group, "We should go and reassure your crew. I am sure they are worried. When we have everyone settled in we will meet in the conference room to come up with a plan to rescue Mary."

X'orige looked at his Co-Commander and said, "Thank you, Amden, I often forget the needs of living beings. I will plot a course to Netula, the planet where we believe Mary is currently located, and will be ready to meet when everyone has taken nourishment and had a rest."

Chapter 25

While the Warship Falconoid was rushing to rescue her Mary was enjoying being taken care of by the Aeroleet. She was still a little weak but she was growing stronger every day. Biz escorted his family home as soon as he was sure Mary was recovering but didn't stay with them because he was anxious to return to Mary. He felt something big was about to happen but he wasn't sure if it was something good.

He watched over Mary, and he worried while he waited. He didn't have to wait long. It was only a few days after his return that he found out that his premonition was right. Something was about to happen that would change their lives yet again.

Mary was much stronger but the Aeroleet insisted that she rest each afternoon. She was napping when she was awakened by a voice inside her head.

Mary?

"What?" she asked sleepily. But there was no one there. "That sounded just like Granny," she said as she sat up, "But how can that be?" She concentrated in the way that Granny had taught her. *Granny, can you hear me?*

Yes my child.

Granny how can it be that you can hear me. You said you wouldn't be able to hear me unless you were near to me, Mary concentrated on asking.

That is true. But I am near. I have traveled a long way to find you and am very close to the planet where you have been stranded.

But how did you get here? Mary asked.

That is a long story, my child. I will tell you all about it when we get there.

When will you be here?

Soon, Mary. Be patient.

Granny?

Yes Mary.

I've missed you.

I've missed you too, Mary.

"Biz! Abarab! Come quickly. I have exciting news!" Mary shouted to her friends.

Biz was the first to reach Mary but Abarab was not far behind.

"Mary, what is all the excitement about?" Abarab said as she floated anxiously near Mary.

"Granny is on her way here to rescue us!" Mary answered excitedly. "I can't believe it. I have so much to do. I have to go back to the cave and activate X'akara so we can prepare to leave."

Abarab waited quietly as Mary bounced up and down in her excitement. She felt sad her friend was about the leave and she was trying hard to hide her feeling of sadness.

It was only a few seconds before Mary noticed Abarab was not sharing her joy.

"Oh, Abarab. I am sorry. My going home would mean I have to leave you," Mary cried as he hugged her friend. "Oh what am I to do?"

Abarab hugged Mary and then said, "I knew you would leave some day, Mary and though it breaks my heart I know you must go. Do not be sad for me. I have my family. You must go to yours."

Mary and Biz left their friends the Aeroleet the next day and journeyed back to the cave. Everything there was as they left it.

"Biz, should I wake X'akara now or wait until Granny gets here?" Mary asked when they had settled in the cave.

Biz just shrugged and settled down on Mary's shoulder.

"You're no help," Mary said. "I think I will wait a little longer. She didn't have much power left."

It would be several days before Granny would be arriving. During the wait Mary was busy packing the things she wanted to take with her and planning a party for their friends the Aeroleet and Biz's family. Mary and Biz went out and searched for the food and prepared it. It was good to have their friends with them and it helped to pass the time.

"I know the food is not as good as yours," Mary said, "But I hope you enjoy it."

Everyone seemed to have a good time, even though they were a little sad.

Mary wanted to communicate more with Granny, but Granny said it was too dangerous and she would explain when she saw Mary.

Shield your thoughts Mary, but listen for my thoughts. I will let you know when we are on our way to the surface.

Very well, Granny. I will try very hard. Mary answered.

Even as busy as she kept herself it seemed a very long time until she heard Granny's message, *Mary we are on our way down to the planet.*

I am near a clearing with a cave high above it. Mary answered. *Do you need any more information?*

"*No, Mary. As long as you have the necklace I gave you we will be able to find you.*

Mary anxiously watched the sky. She could barely stand still as she waited. It wasn't long before she could see a tiny speck in the sky streaking toward her and she exclaimed, "Oh, Biz, there is the shuttle. I can't wait!" Then she rushed into the cave to activate X'akara.

X'akara powered up and then said, "Is there something wrong? Why have you activated me?"

Mary smiled at the CAMCIA and said, "Nothing is wrong. Everything is wonderfully right! We are about to be rescued! Granny felt my anxiety all the way to New Quain and she organized a rescue party. The shuttle coming in for a landing now."

X'akara got up slowly and went to the mouth of the cave and looked up at the approaching shuttle. "How could Granny organize a rescue party?

"I don't know. We will just have to ask Granny when she gets here. Come on X'akara, they are almost down. I can't wait to see Granny again!"

Biz was thrilled that Mary was happy and buzzed excitedly about her head. They ran down to the landing site and waited until the shuttle came to a halt in the same clearing where they had crash-landed. X'akara arrived just before the outer door opened and Granny stepped out to greet Mary.

Mary was hugging Granny and Arman when X'orige stepped out of the shuttle.

"Father!" she shouted. "You're alive!"

X'orige stood for a moment, before he answered. "X'akara, have you not informed this child that we are not her parents and that we are CAMCIA?"

"Of course, X'orige," X'akara answered, "But I understand the child's puzzlement. How is it that you were not destroyed?"

Before X'orige could answer Mary ran to him and hugged him and said, "Oh, I know you are not alive as I am alive, but I was so excited to see you that I forgot for a minute. How did you get here with Granny? How did you survive the explosion and get away from the Bahadin?"

X'orige stood assessing the child in front of him and said, "I will answer your questions in due time and I have questions as well but now we need to prepare to depart. The window of time for our best trajectory to the ship is narrow."

Mary rushed about gathering the things she wanted to take with her and was ready to depart when Abarab and the Aeroleet arrived along with Biz's family. Mary went to each individual and said goodbye, leaving Abarab until the last.

"Abarab, how can I say goodbye? You saved my life and my sanity. It is almost more than I can stand to leave you."

"I know Mary. I will miss you," Abarab said and then turned away unable to say any more.

Biz was busy saying goodbye to his family and the air was filled with the sad chirps of the barda.

Above the noise X'orige shouted, "We must depart now. Please, Mary and X'akara, come inside!"

Mary climbed the ramp and sadly turned one more time to wave at her friends. Her eyes blurred with tears she said, "Why am I always saying goodbye?" and ran up the ramp into the shuttle. Moments later the shuttle departed for the ship.

"X'akara," X'orige said as they traveled to the Falconoid, "There is something that I must tell you and the child before we reach the ship. Do not be alarmed when you see that it is a Bahadin Warship. We disarmed the Bahadin and took over the ship. The Bahadin who commanded it are our prisoners and are being held in the slave quarters."

"My goodness, X'orige! You are my hero. Please tell me how you managed to do that all by yourself!" X'akara said in a little girl voice filled with awe.

X'orige turned to face X'akara and said, "What is wrong with your voice?"

"Mary has been teaching me to have some personality," she answered demurely.

"Well, my dear, this is truly an interesting development," X'orige said in a deep masculine voice tinged with laughter, "I too have been learning to have more personality."

Mary giggled at the antics of the CAMCIA and sighed as she thought, "Too bad they didn't act like that when we were posing as a family back on Earth. I think I would have had a lot more fun."

The ride in the shuttle was smooth and fast. In no time they were approaching the Falconoid. "Look Mary, there is the ship," X'orige said pointing to the location of the warship."

Mary was amazed by the size of the Falconoid. "Wow! That thing is huge!" she exclaimed, "I thought our old ship was big, but this is unbelievable."

"Yes it is quite large and powerful. It will be of great benefit to all that fight against the evil Bahadin," X'orige answered.

When the shuttle was safely docked and secured X'orige opened the hatch and the passengers disembarked. Mary was half way across the bay when she noticed that she was walking on the floor. "Wait a minute," she exclaimed, What's going on here? I thought we were in space."

"We are, Mary." X'orige answered, "You could see that from the shuttle's windows."

"But that's impossible. I'm walking on the floor," she said, "How can that be. There is no gravity in space."

"This ship is equipped with artificial gravity. It is not perfect, some of the outer corridors have less gravity than the inner segments but it is much more comfortable for humans on long trips." X'orige answered. "Of course I have no problem with weightlessness."

Granny walked up beside Mary and put an arm around her and said, "Well, I for one appreciate this artificial gravity. Weightlessness makes me dizzy sometimes."

"Oh I didn't have any problems after I got used to it and sometimes I had fun bouncing around. But if it makes you feel better, Granny, I am glad this ship has it," Mary said as she walked with Granny to the lift that would take them to their quarters.

Biz who had gotten over his melancholy, buzzed about happily chirping. He was happy to be with Mary and could feel her excitement.

Mary's quarters on the ship were small but comfortable. It had a bed on one side of the compartment that folded into the wall when not in use and a small desk and chair that also folded into a cabinet on the opposite side. There was a small closet for Mary's clothes in which she lovingly placed her one remaining dress from New Quain.

"I wish I had been able to save my other clothes," Mary told Biz with a sigh.

Biz landed on her shoulder and cooed softly. Then he pulled a strand of Mary's hair and flew just out of her reach.

"Biz, you rascal!" Mary said, "I can't play now because I have to get ready for transition. We will play when I wake up."

Biz chirped and settled in Mary's pocket as she pulled out her bed.

They didn't have to wait long for the signal that the ship was about to transition into hypervelocity. Mary experienced only minor discomfort much to her surprise.

"Wow Biz, that was the easiest transition I have gone through," Mary said to Biz who never seemed to experience any discomfort at all. Biz chirped happily and buzzed Mary's head.

"Alright, I'll play with you now," she said as she jumped up and began chasing the barda around the chamber. As usual she was unable to catch him and she collapsed, giggling on her bed. "Biz," she said breathlessly, "You are just too good. I can't catch you."

Biz hovered just out of reach taunting her with his chirps and flying in closer only to quickly move away when Mary attempted to catch him.

"Ok, I give up, she said and pretended to ignore him.

Biz cautiously moved in closer but still Mary didn't look at him. He became careless and moved closer still. Then with a quick move Mary caught her little playmate in her hand.

"Fooled you, didn't I, she said with a grin," she said but she knew Biz wasn't that easy to fool. He snuggled against her hand and chirped softly.

"You let me catch you, didn't you?" Mary said as she softly caressed his tiny head.

Biz looked up at Mary with his sweetest innocent expression and nuzzled her hand.

Mary quickly adjusted to life aboard the ship and being with Granny again was wonderful. They sat for hours talking and Mary began to realize just how much she had missed Granny. During one of their visits Granny was talking about going to Ayri and how excited Mary must be to finally meet her parents when Mary began to cry.

"What's wrong, Mary?" Granny asked gathering the sobbing child into her arms.

"Granny, I'm so scared. What if my parents don't like me?"

"Now, now child. Don't worry. They love you. Remember the dreams of your mother. That was her love reaching out to you."

"But what if she is disappointed in me. I don't know how to be a princess. What if everyone on Ayri finds out I am just an ordinary kid."

"Mary, you are not just an ordinary kid. You are very special. You have an inner strength that is far stronger than your power as a Thayer and you are an extremely powerful Thayer," Granny said as she comforted Mary.

"But Granny, I don't know how to act or what to say," Mary said.

"Don't worry. When the time comes you will know. I have faith in you," Granny said with assurance, "Now dry your eyes. Why don't you go and see what Arman and X'orige are up to in the control room."

When she reached the control room Amden, Arman and X'orige were studying the navigational display screen.

"What are you guys doing?" Mary asked.

Arman turned with a smile and said, "Hi Mary. We were trying to figure out how we are going to get past the Bahadin Battleships surrounding Ayri and the Ayri defense system. I think we can bluff our way through the battleships but an impenetrable force shield surrounds Ayri. If we manage to get past the force shield the Ayri defense system will probably try to shoot us down, not knowing we are not actually Bahadin. Quite a problem huh?"

"Why don't you just tell them that we have captured the Bahadin Ship?" Mary asked.

"I doubt that they would believe us, Mary," Amden answered, "I wish it was that easy."

"Wait a minute, look at this!" Amden exclaimed pointing at the screen. "There is a gap in the force shield in this area."

Arman and X'orige gathered around and stared at the spot Amden indicated. "Yes," X'orige said, "But it is not large enough for the ship to get through."

"No, Its not," Amden said with a grin, "But a shuttle could get through."

X'orige paused a moment and then said, "Yes, the gap is large enough for the shuttle but I know this area. It is in the most desolate region of the planet, a harsh lifeless desert. If we did manage to slip the shuttle through the gap it would most likely be caught in one of the many fierce storms that rage there. If we managed to get past the storms then the defense system surrounding the parameter of the desert would surely destroy the shuttle."

"But," Amden said pausing for emphasis, "What if we go through the gap, staying high enough to avoid the storms and then before we reach the parameter land and walk into this city."

"What city?" X'orige asked.

"This one right here," Amden said pointing at the screen.

"That's Tacama," X'orige said, "It's an outpost defense station. You wouldn't like it there. The inhabitants are rough and uncivilized. Only the toughest soldiers are stationed there and the citizens that choose to live there are mostly criminals and thieves. It is a hard place and violence is a way of life. There is no law there except the survival of the fittest."

"Perfect!" said Amden with a grin, "They will never notice a few more criminals in a place like that."

"You can't be serious," Arman and X'orige shouted at once.

"Yes, I am. It is perfect. They won't be expecting anybody to come in from the desert. We will be there and gone before anyone knows what happened."

X'orige studied the screen for a few minutes and then much to Arman and Amden's surprise said, "I have considered all the factors and possibilities and I have concluded that this is our only choice. It will be difficult and dangerous and we should begin making our plans immediately."

Mary slipped quietly out of the control room and rushed to Granny's compartment. When she got there she found Granny packing her things.

"Granny," Mary said breathlessly, "They have figured out how to get down to the planet!"

"I know," Granny said, "I heard every word."

"But how, Granny," Mary questioned, "You weren't there."

"Mary, I heard your thoughts. Have you completely forgotten how to shield your thoughts?"

Mary paused and stammered, "I ah, Oh my goodness, I guess I did forget to shield my thoughts."

"Mary, listen carefully to me. You must shield your thoughts at all times, especially now that we are nearing Ayri. We don't know if there are other traitors among your people and until we can get you safely to your family you will have to shield every thought all the time. Do you understand?"

Granny looked very stern and Mary was upset that she had disappointed her friend. "I'm sorry," she cried, "I will try harder."

Granny took Mary into her arms and comforted her as she said, "Hush Mary, don't cry. I know it is hard for you. I sometimes forget that being a Thayer is new to you. You have not had the years of practice that make shielding easy for most Thayers. I will work with you in the time remaining and we will practice. Now here take my handkerchief and dry your eyes."

Mary wiped her eyes and said with a trembling voice, "Thank you Granny. I am sorry I disappointed you and I hope you are not still mad at me."

"Oh Mary, I was never angry with you. I only spoke so harshly because I am afraid for you. I love you child."

"I love you too, Granny and I promise that I will practice very hard."

"I know you will child," Granny said and sighed. She managed to smile as she released Mary in spite of her own tears that threatened to fall.

The ship transitioned out of hypervelocity in an area far from the normal transition site to avoid contact with the Bahadin. Then they made a long circuitous approach to the planet that would bring them to the area of the gap without encountering any other Warships.

The next day Amden, Arman, X'akara and X'orige called a meeting to discuss their plans. They had worked long hours deciding who would go to the surface and what supplies would be needed.

When everyone was seated in the meeting room X'orige stood before the assembled group and announced, "As many of you know we are in stationary orbit above the planet Ayri. We have found an opening in the shield in this sector," he said pointing to the map of the planet below that was displayed on the viewing screen. "The hole in the shield is only large enough for a shuttle to pass through. Therefore we are limited in the number of people and the amount of supplies we can transport. This part of the planet is a desolate area of unpopulated desert wasteland so we should be able to land undetected. Arman and X'akara will lead the expedition and Amden and I will remain on the ship. When you have landed you will disembark and proceed to Tacama. We have decided that it would best if you travel on the outskirts of the outpost and avoid contact with the locals. X'akara will go into Tacama and attempt to purchase some type of transport. Then you will proceed as quickly as possible to Merald. Are there any questions?"

"How much time do we have before we depart for the surface?" Granny asked.

X'orige turned to face Granny and said, "We have enough time to pack our supplies and have a short rest. It will not take long to travel through the gap and down to the surface."

"I am already packed and ready so I will help Mary get ready," Granny said, "Come on Mary, lets get busy packing your things."

"Wait, Granny," Arman said, "I'm sorry but you must stay here."

"What? That's ridiculous!" Granny exclaimed, "Who decided that?"

"We decided that you should stay here," Arman said, "It is going to be very hard traveling across the desert and forgive me but, Granny you are not as young as you used to be. Besides we need you here."

"Oh, You think I am too feeble, do you!" Granny said gritting her teeth, "I can out last any of you young pups. Besides, Mary needs me. She is a powerful Thayer, but she lacks control. Do you think any of you have more experience in training a Thayer?"

Arman hesitated for a moment and then spoke, "Maybe you are right, Granny. She could use help in controlling her powers. Amden, X'orige, I think Granny may prove more useful than me, so I will remain on board the ship."

"But," Amden said choosing his words carefully, "Do you really think Granny will able to withstand the treacherous desert crossing, not to mention traveling cross country to Merald?"

"She is much stronger than she appears," Arman said with a grin, "She has proved that to me many times. I find it is much easier to do as she says."

"So it is set then," X'orige said, "Mary, Granny, X'akara, and Amden will be the landing party. One of our CAMCIA pilots will fly the shuttle to the surface and return to the ship. X'akara has prepared a list of supplies and will have them loaded on the shuttle and we will send the clothing you need to your compartments. It is important that you dress properly especially for the trek through the desert. Does anyone have any questions? No? Then try to get some rest until the shuttle is ready."

Mary walked with Granny to her chamber. "You don't have to help me pack. I am only taking a few things. Why don't you go and rest. We probably won't have much time to rest when we get to the surface."

Granny smiled and hugged Mary. "Alright I will try to rest."

Inside her chamber Mary tried to take a nap but she was too nervous. Biz tried to calm her, but it was no use. Finally she got up, dressed in what she now thought of as her 'desert wear'. X'akara had sent detailed instructions on how to put on in the outfit.

1. Put on the pants and long sleeved turtleneck shirt being careful to tuck the shirttail into the pants.
2. Put on the socks and pull up over the pants.
3. Pull on the long boots.
4. Put on the long tunic, secured in the front.

"Well this certainly is a strange outfit to wear in the desert!" Mary thought as she finished dressing, "But at least there is a pocket inside for you, Biz."

Biz inspected his pocket and apparently found it satisfactory because he settled down and went to sleep.

I wish I were as calm as he is, Mary thought to herself.

Mary gathered a few things she wanted to take with her and made her way to the shuttle. When she got there she found she was not the only one unable to rest.

“Granny, why aren’t you resting?” Mary asked.

“Oh, I suppose for the same reason you’re not resting. I couldn’t lie still. I decided I would bring my things to the shuttle and wait for everyone here.”

“Me too. I am excited and scared and oh, I don’t know what,” Mary said as she looked inside the shuttle.

They were busy inspecting the shuttle when Amden stuck his head inside.

“You couldn’t rest either, huh?” He said with a smile. I think we should find X’akara and get going. No use waiting around is there?”

X’akara was not pleased that they had not rested as instructed. “You have a long hard trip in front of you and you may be sorry you didn’t rest when you had the chance. But, since you seem to be anxious to be on your way we will go as soon as I make sure you have dressed according to my specifications.”

X'akara checked each person and said, "I see everyone has heeded my instructions. If you are sure you don't want to wait we will prepare to depart for the surface."

"X'akara," Mary asked, "Is it very cold where we are going? I thought deserts were hot places."

"It is very hot during the day in the desert and only slightly cooler at night," X'akara answered.

"But," Mary said looking down at the clothing that completely covered her from head to foot, "Why are we dressed in all these clothes?"

"The cloth next to your skin absorbs sweat and keeps you comfortable even in the highest temperatures and your skin needs to be covered to prevent burning from the suns and to protect it during sand storms. The boots come up high because it will keep the sand out when you are walking in deep sand."

It wasn't long before they were buckled in and ready to go to the surface. Mary held Granny's hand as the shuttle slowly moved out of the bay and accelerated toward the surface. Even with Mary's thoughts shielded Granny could still feel her excitement.

Chapter 26

The shuttle exited the docking bay and out into the darkness of space. The planet below seemed small at first but grew larger as they got closer. Mary was looking out the porthole and it occurred to her that she couldn't see a shield around the planet.

"Amden, I thought you said there was a shield. I don't see anything."

Amden unbuckled and slid over to Mary and pointed to a spot just above the horizon and said, "See that faint shimmer just where the light meets the darkness?"

"I think so," Mary answered.

"Well, that is about all you can see with the naked eye. The only accurate way to find the shield is with the ship's sensors."

"Oh, alright, I guess," Mary said, "I hope you have good sensors on this shuttle."

"Yes, the Bahadin made excellent sensors. We won't have any problems finding the shield's gap," Amden said with a smile.

"Amden," X'akara said when she noticed he had unbuckled his restraint, "Please go back to your seat and fasten your restraints. We are about the enter the gap."

"0ops, she caught me. I better go back to my seat," Amden said with a chuckle.

The trip through the gap was uneventful and the ride was smooth. Far down below they could seen a massive billowing cloud.

"What is that big gray thing down there?" Mary asked.

X'akara glanced out the porthole and answered, "It appears to be a sandstorm, a meteorological phenomenon that is quite common in this area. It will help hide our landing but I suggest that everyone tighten their restraints as it will be turbulent inside the storm."

Mary tightened her harness and watched through the porthole as they descended into the storm. The sky had lightened as they entered the atmosphere but began to darken as they entered the storm cloud. Soon Mary could see nothing but swirling masses of gray through the porthole.

The shuttle was tossed about and everyone had to hold on for dear life. The closer they got to the ground the worse the winds battered the shuttle and Mary wondered how the pilot could control the ship. Suddenly with a jolt the shuttle was on the ground.

It took a moment for the passengers to realize they were safely on the ground.

"Whew!" Mary exclaimed, "That was scary."

She hardly noticed the increasing pull of gravity during the jolting ride to the surface, but now when she raised her arms she felt as they were made of lead. She reached down and unbuckled her harness and attempted to stand.

"This is harder than I remembered."

"Yes Mary," X'akara said, "it should be. The gravitational pull here is stronger than the artificial gravity on the ship. We must hurry before the shuttle's presence is detected."

"I thought the storm would hide us," Mary said.

"It will to a certain extent but even this fierce storm can not hide our shuttle indefinitely. Also, these storms are unpredictable and may end as suddenly as they appear," X'akara said.

As the rest of the passengers released their harnesses and slowly stood inside the shuttle X'akara was busy preparing to go out into the storm.

"Here, take these and wrap them around your mouths and noses and put these goggles to protect your eyes," X'akara said handing the equipment to Mary, Granny and Amden, "They will help when we get outside in the storm."

They gathered their supplies and wrapped the scarves around their faces, put on the goggles and opened the shuttle door. A blast of hot air filled with blowing sand came howling in the opening. They hurriedly exited the shuttle and struggled out into the storm. They moved away from the shuttle quickly and they could barely hear the engines beginning to rev up in preparation for takeoff. They were soon enveloped in the storm and the sand made it almost impossible to see more than a few inches ahead.

X'akara looped a rope around each of them and warned, "Be very careful and hold on to the rope. If you become separated from the group it will be impossible to find you."

The group struggled behind X'akara, just barely managing to keep up. The sand quickly penetrated the scarves and into their mouths and eyes. None of them were able to tell where they were going but X'akara's guidance system kept them moving in the right direction. Silently they trudged though the shifting sand with their heads bowed concentrating on staying upright and holding on to their rope lifeline.

After a very long time the winds began to gradually die down and visibility improved. When at last the wind completely stopped blowing they removed their goggles and wiped the sand from their eyes. It was the first time they had a good look at their surroundings. They were standing on the top of a large dune surrounded by a sea of sand stretching out in all directions with no sign of life.

"Are you sure we are headed in the right direction?" Mary asked.

"Yes, we are heading in the right direction," X'akara answered, "We will be able to see the outpost soon. I'm sorry we had to walk so far but it would have been dangerous to land any closer. Now we must continue. It is not safe to linger in this desert."

Mary group trudged on but walking in the deep sand was difficult and she had to work very hard to lift her foot from the sand. On each step her foot seemed to sink deeper into the sand. Then suddenly she wasn't able to lift her foot at all and she fell face forward in the sand.

"Help me," she screamed as she felt something pull her foot deeper into the sand.

X'akara upon hearing Mary's cry turned around to see Mary's legs disappearing into the sand. She moved quickly to Mary's side, grabbed her leg and shouted to Amden, "Quick, take your knife and cut the tentacle when I pull her foot out."

Amden took his knife from its sheath and ran to Mary's side. He gasped in horror as he saw the large gray rope-like tentacle that was wrapped around Mary's boot.

"Amden, be very careful not to touch the flesh of the tentacle as you cut it," X'akara instructed as she struggled to keep the tentacle from pulling Mary's foot into the sand, "The tentacle will cause a severe burn if it touches your bare skin."

Amden valiantly sawed at the appendage but cutting the tentacle was difficult and he hacked with all his might at the tough flesh until finally he was able to cut though it. The main tentacle slithered back down into the sand leaving a trail of black fluid. The end of the tentacle was still wrapped tightly around Mary's boot and X'akara slowly removed it.

"Thank you, X'akara. I thought you were being foolish about wearing all these clothes, but you were right," Mary said as she shakily stood up, "Lets get out of here before whatever that thing was decides to grab me again!"

They continued on stopping only briefly for food and water. Mary was wondering how much longer they had to walk when far in the distance she saw a flash of light. Soon she could see the shapes of buildings far ahead.

"We should reach the outskirts just before dark," X'akara said as they walked toward the outpost.

Soon the light began fading and all was dark in the desert. They were very near to the outpost and the glow of the lights from the outpost appeared inviting but they knew they couldn't go into the settlement.

"This is as close as you should be," X'akara said, "Wait here while I go and find a vehicle."

"X'akara, what about that thing that grabbed my foot? Are there any of them here?" Mary asked anxiously.

"No, I believe they stay away from settlements," X'akara answered. "Stay hidden and don't move until I get back."

Mary was very tired and slowly sat down but she was unable to relax because she kept imagining tentacles reaching up to drag her down into the sand. Biz wiggled inside Mary's pocket and she realized that he probably was tired of being cooped up. She reached inside her tunic and brought out her little friend. He stretched his tiny wings and flew up above Mary's head.

"Now don't go flying off Biz. I don't want you to get lost from me."

Biz chirped softly and seemed content to stay close to Mary and only flew in circles around her to exercise his wings after the long day inside the pocket. He could sense her uneasiness and landed often on her shoulder to reassure her.

They sat in the cool night for a very long time and Mary was becoming anxious.

"Granny, I'm worried about X'akara. Shouldn't she have been back by now?" Mary asked.

"I'm sure she is alright." Granny answered, "X'akara is quite capable of taking care of herself."

Mary sighed and tried to relax. She was so very tired after the long walk through the desert. Biz settled down on her shoulder and Mary drifted off into an uneasy sleep.

She was dreaming about giant bees when she awoke with a start and shook her head. She was still hearing the drone of the bees. She looked around and saw X'akara drive over the top of the dune in a very unusual vehicle.

"Where in this forsaken place did you find that piece of junk?" Amden asked when X'akara jumped down from the craft.

"I am sorry it does not meet with your approval Amden," X'akara said, "It was the only transport I could find that was for sale."

Mary could only stare openmouthed at the strange object before her. It was shaped roughly like a large topless box resting on two misshapen skids. The sides were covered with large dents, holes and rust. The paint that remained was a sickly brownish yellow with a slight tinge of green. A plaque on the side proclaimed the vehicle to be a Regal 200 All Terrain Hovercraft Transport System under which someone had painted the word "RAT", obviously a name taken from the initials of the craft. Two doors along the side of the vehicle appeared to have been welded shut. A shredded canopy attached to twisted framework was partially extended over the compartment. When Mary climbed up over the side of the vehicle she saw benches covered with filthy tattered pillows. It was not exactly the type of transportation she had envisioned.

X'akara helped Granny climb up into the vehicle and then she and Amden began loading their supplies. When they were all seated Amden went to the front of the vehicle and looked at the controls.

"I'll be surprised if this thing makes it to Merald!" Amden said.

X'akara joined Amden at the front of the vehicle and said, "This transport does look bad on the outside but I examined the engine and it appears to be in excellent shape.

"Is the directional equipment calibrated?" Amden asked, "We will have to depend on it to get to Merald. We won't have the luxury of skyways out here."

"I believe the directional equipment is in working order. I checked it against my internal system on the way here. I think this vehicle must have belonged to a smuggler who deliberately distressed the outside to blend in with the locals."

"Well I hope you are right," Amden said as X'akara moved the lever forward and the craft rose slightly and began to move forward, "Hey, it is as quiet as this type vehicle gets and it appears to be moving smoothly. Maybe you were right."

After they got underway X'akara let Amden take the controls and turned to Mary and Granny and said," We will be traveling through a sparsely inhabited part of the world, during the first part of our journey, but we still do not want to draw any attention to ourselves. If we encounter any people we will pose as a farm family on our way to visit family in Merald. I have chosen names typical for a farm family from Ayri for you. Granny, you will be Mary's grandmother S'mer, Amden will be S'den Mary's brother, and Mary will be S'mary."

"What name did you give yourself, X'akara?" Mary asked.

"There is no need to change my name. I already have a typical name for a CAMCIA."

They traveled on through the night and into the next day without any trouble. Mary sat transfixed watching the countryside flying by. The RAT ran remarkably smoothly hovering just above the ground as it sped along.

During the night they has passed through the outskirts of the desert and into a lush forest. The tall trees were very similar to the trees that Mary remembered from Earth. It was comforting to have something familiar. Then the land changed yet again with long stretches of flat lands. There were two suns that rose from opposite sides of the skies of Ayri. One was much larger and closer while the other was weaker and appeared to be very small. It was felt odd at first to have sunlight coming from two directions but after several days she hardly noticed.

X'akara was pleased that they were making good time and believed if nothing happened they would arrive in Merald in a few more days. Mary was excited and scared. She was still worried that her family wouldn't want her and yet she longed to see them.

Chapter 27

They were less than two days from Merald when the RAT began to fail. First it was just a small vibration but soon the vibration became much more noticeable. They only hoped it would hold out until they reached Merald but then with a loud bang and a puff of acid smoke the RAT ground to a stop.

X'akara climbed down from the RAT and began to inspect the engine. Amden stood close by watching. Mary and Granny Mer climbed down and sat on the ground under the shade of a large tree. The day had become very warm and they both were very sleepy. Within a few minutes they were sound asleep. Biz snuggled inside Mary's pocket and soon he too fell asleep.

X'akara and Amden were so engrossed in the RAT's repairs that they didn't notice a man and a child walking across the large field where the RAT had come to rest.

"You people having a problem with your transport?" the man asked startling Amden.

Amden turned to see a large man and a small child smiling at him. "Yes," he managed to say as he gathered his wits, "It started vibrating and then quit with a bang."

"My name is S'ramo and this is my daughter S'rybe. We live just over there," the man said pointing back across the field, "I used to tinker with these things. Mind if I have a look at it?"

Amden smiled at the man and said, "I am S'den and this is our CAMCIA X'akara. Our Grandmother S'mer and my sister S'mary are resting under the tree. We would appreciate any help you can give us. I can't seem to find the problem," Amden answered with a smile.

As the adults worked on the vehicle S'rybe grew bored and walked over to where Mary slept. She wished the girl would wake up. She didn't get to see many other children because she lived so far out in the country.

Maybe if I just wiggle her foot a little she will wake up, S'rybe thought as she reached for Mary's foot.

Mary awoke to find a child staring intently at her. At first she was too surprised to say anything but then she remembered her manners and said, "Contenza."

"Contenza. I am glad to see you are awake. I wanted to talk to you. You see I don't get to see any other children very often. My name is S'rybe. That man over there said your name was S'mary. Would you like to play with me? I like to play. Maybe you can come and play at my house. We could have a really good time."

Mary sat and listened in amazement as the girl in front of her babbled on. She had never encountered someone so talkative before.

"My parents say I talk too much. You don't think I talk too much do you? I don't think so. I have to be by myself so much that when I do see someone to talk to I have a lot to say."

S'rybe continued to talk and Mary found that all she needed to do was nod her head occasionally. She wondered how long the child could keep talking and she was having a hard time concentrating on what she was saying. Mary didn't want to be impolite.

Some time during S'rybe's speech Granny awoke and sat up.

S'rybe paused briefly and turned to Granny and said, "Contenza, Grandmother of S'mary. My name is S'rybe. I have been talking with S'mary. I hope I didn't wake you with all my talk. My father says I talk too much but I don't think I talk too much. I just have a lot to say."

Biz was still asleep inside Mary's pocket when S'rybe walked up. S'rybe's constant chatter woke him. He stretched and stuck out his head to see what was going on. He smiled at the child and climbed out of Mary's pocket and flew over for a closer look.

"Tra! Is that a real barda?" S'rybe exclaimed. "I never saw a real one before. I read about them. I wanted one but my parents said that you don't get a barda, they get you. Is that right? Did this one get you? Mother said she knew someone who had one once. He is so cute. Can I touch him?"

Mary smiled and said "If he will let you. Just hold out your hand and if he likes you he will land on it."

S'rybe held out her hand and Biz with a chirp landed on her outstretched hand. He accepted with pleasure the gentle stroke of S'rybe's hand and began softly chirping, closing his eyes in contentment.

"I think he likes you," Mary said.

At this point S'rybe's father walked over and put his hand on her shoulder. "Contenza, my name is S'ramo. I hope my daughter has not been bothering you."

Granny could feel the love the father and child shared and she smiled and said, "Contenza, S'ramo. You have a lovely daughter and she has been entertaining us. Isn't that right S'mary?"

"Yes, she surely has been entertaining," Mary answered with a grin. "Is she always this ah -," Mary stammered, unable to come up with a polite word.

"Talkative?" S'ramo said completing the sentence for Mary. "Yes she is except when she is asleep. Please forgive her for bothering you. She is a good child."

"There is nothing to forgive," Granny said, "She has been entertaining and very polite. And see how the barda has accepted her. That means that she must be a good person. Barda are very good judges of character.

S'ramo smiled with pleasure at the compliment to his child and then said, "Thank you for your kind words. But I am forgetting what I came over to tell you. The RAT can be repaired but it will take quite a while. I would like to invite you to come to my home to rest and have some food while your CAMCIA finishes the repairs."

"Thank you. We would be honored to accept your hospitality," Granny said.

"No it is I that am honored," S'ramo said, "My home is just over there beyond the trees. I will go ahead to make arrangements and you may come at your leisure."

"Now S'rybe, give the barda back to Mary. We most go tell your Mother we have guests," S'ramo said as he picked up S'rybe, placed her on his shoulders and walked quickly away.

S'rybe turned around and shouted, "Come quickly. I want to talk to you some more." Then more quietly she said to her father, "I like them."

S'ramo smiled and thought to himself, *If S'rybe likes them then they must be good people. She has never been wrong about anyone.*

Mary and Granny agreed that S'ramo and S'rybe were good and kind. They both felt sincerity and kindness radiating from the father and daughter.

"I could feel S'rybe reaching out to me mentally and I answered with similar feeling. It was hard to hold back, though," Mary said.

"I know," Granny said, "I could feel it too. You were right to hold back. She is a small child and you may have injured her if you weren't shielded."

"Do you really think so?" Mary asked.

"Yes, my child, I do. You have an awesome power that you have only partially tapped. I hope you never have to fully unleash it."

"Mary! Granny!" Amden shouted to them, "X'akara said she will finish the work on the RAT by herself. Come on let's go get some food and a little rest while we can."

"We will be right there," Mary answered"

Mary and Granny went to the RAT and collected some of their things.

"X'akara, please let us know as soon as you have finished fixing the RAT," Amden said as they walked away.

"Of course," X'akara answered, without removing her head from inside the panel of the RAT, "It shouldn't be long. S'ramo saved us a lot of time searching for the problem with his extensive knowledge of the mechanics of the RAT."

Mary, Granny and Amden walked across the field in the direction that S'ramo and S'rybe had taken. The air was warm in the glow of the two suns and Mary tried to enjoy the beauty of the land around her, but she was so tired. *How much further is it,* she thought.

"Where is their house?" she asked. It was a struggle to keep putting one foot in front of the other.

"It's right in front of us," Amden answered, "Can't you see it?"

"Where?" Mary asked unable to see anything that resembled a house. All that was in front of them was a large hill covered with flowers, "Do we have to climb or go around that hill?"

"That 'hill' is a structure called a marhom and it is their house, Mary. That is now they build them here. It protects them from the fierce storms that sweep across this area during the change of seasons. The wind flows right over the rounded shape without causing any damage and they are very energy efficient."

"Oh," Mary said staring at the 'hill', "How did you know that Amden? I thought you had never been here before."

"My planet traded with Ayri before the war with the Bahadin. Our engineers did an extensive study on the marhom structures. I was studying to be an engineer when the Bahadin captured me." Amden walked on with his head bowed as the memories of his lost home threatened to overwhelm him.

He looked so dejected that Mary ran to his side and took his hand. "Amden, I'm sorry," she cried, "I didn't mean to bring back sad memories to you."

Amden looked down at Mary and smiled, "It's alright, Mary. It does hurt to think of the hopes and dreams that I had back then. I will always miss my family and friends that I loved and lost forever that day and I don't want to forget them even if it makes me sad to think of them. Don't worry. I will be all right."

Mary hugged Amden and wiped away her tears. She took Amden's hand and they walked slowly toward the marhom.

When they reached the marhom S'rybe and S'ramo were waiting by the door. "Welcome to our home", S'ramo said with a bow, "Please come inside and meet my wife, S'ube. S'ube this is Granny Mer, Amden and Mary."

Mary gasped as she realized that S'ramo had introduced them by their real names, "How did you know our names?"

"S'rybe told us your names. She has a talent for finding a person's true name, along with her other talents," S'ramo answered with a smile and bowing low again he said, "But, please don't linger on the door step, come inside and do not be afraid. S'rybe also told us you are good and kind people even though you gave us false names. She is never wrong."

Mary, Granny and Amden walked into the cool comfort to the marhom. Mary looked around in amazement. The room was large with a domed-shaped ceiling high above. The white walls were decorated with large mosaic murals. Two of the murals depicted farm life and the others pictured the views outside the marhom. The floor was covered with polished stone tiles with thick rugs scattered about. A huge fireplace encased in glass covered one entire wall of the room. An enormous round table was located in the center of the room. Circular padded benches surrounded it.

"Mary," S'rybe said taking Mary's hand, "Come, let me show you my dolls."

Mary followed S'rybe to the area in front of the fireplace and sat down on a large comfortable pillow. As they sat on the rug S'rybe introduced Mary to each of her dolls.

"This is S'abbe and this one is S'balie and this one is S'orbie. I have more dolls in my room. We'll go and play with them later. Mother won't let me bring all of them out here at one time. She says it makes too much clutter. I don't think of it as clutter, but you know how mothers are."

Then, as S'rybe continued to talk in a steady stream, a large primitive CAMCIA rolled through a door and scanned the room. When he had located S'ube and S'ramo he rolled over to them and slowly said in a tinny voice, "I…numbered…the persons. I…am ready…to prepare food…at…your…command."

"Thank you X'E57, "S'ube said, "Prepare the food now."

"You…are…welcome…" X'E57 said and rolled quietly out of the room.

"Our CAMCIA is old and doesn't have a large vocabulary but he is an excellent cook," S'ube said.

Soon X'E57 returned with a steaming platter of food that filled the room with a delicious aroma. He placed the platter on the table and left the room again. He returned with a stack of eating vessels and utensils.

While everyone else in the room was watching the CAMCIA set the table Mary and S'rybe played quietly with the dolls.

"I have never had a doll." Mary said.

"What? Never had a doll? That is hard to believe since you are…" S'rybe said.

"Since I am what?" Mary asked.

"You know," S'rybe said leaning closer and whispering "The Heir Apparent."

"Oh, no!" Mary said.

"Oh yes! I know who you are," S'rybe said.

"How did you know that?"

"I can tell lots of things about people, even if they are shielded. It drives my parents crazy," S'rybe said. "It gets me in trouble sometimes, too."

"But, I wasn't thinking about that. How could you tell?"

"I don't know. Sometimes things just pop in my head. Maybe someone else was thinking about it."

Mary watched as S'rybe picked up one of the dolls and held it close. She had the feeling that S'rybe was troubled about something.

"S'rybe, is something bothering you?"

"Yes. It's none of my business but I was wondering why are you riding around in a beat up old RAT and calling yourself Mary? Shouldn't you be at the palace with your family? I mean, well everybody knows it is a dangerous time and, uh—," S'rybe stuttered, her face turning red.

"What?" Mary asked.

"I didn't know there was an Heir Apparent."

"Nobody is supposed to know. My Mother sent me away to a secret place to protect me from the Bahadin but they found me. When they attacked my hiding place I had to leave in a hurry and I have been trying to get back here every since. It's a long story."

MARY! STOP! YOU MUST NOT SAY ANYMORE! Mary grabbed her head as the thought from Granny exploded in her brain.

Granny it is all right. She already knows who I am. There is no keeping it from her. Besides, I have a strong feeling I can trust her, Mary projected to Granny.

There was no answer but Mary could feel that Granny was worried.

The ancient CAMCIA finished setting the table and announced "Your…Nourishment…is ready…to be…consumed."

"Come on, Mary, lets get some food," S'rybe said taking Mary's hand, "I can't wait to tell them who you are. They will be surprised!"

Mary jumped up, pulled S'rybe around and said, "Don't tell anyone who I am."

"But, I have to tell my parents. I can't hide anything from them."

"Please, S'rybe, don't tell them or anyone. I am begging you."

"OK," S'rybe said with a troubled look on her face, "but they will kill me when they find out."

"If they find out you can say it was my fault because I told you not to tell."

S'rybe grinned mischievously and said in a whisper, "Yea, they can't punish me for obeying an order from the Heir Apparent!"

"Stop calling me that," Mary whispered, "Remember it is our secret."

"Yes Mary," S'rybe said a little too loudly and then in a whisper, "but you have to promise to tell me everything later."

The food was excellent but Mary was too nervous to eat. She wanted to talk to Granny about what happened but she couldn't while they were eating.

Oh, what am I to do? She thought, *I'm afraid I can't trust S'rybe to keep my secret.*

S'rybe turned to Mary and smiled. She pulled Mary close and whispered, "Don't worry, I won't tell."

"But, how did you know what I was thinking?"

"Told you, I know what people think."

Mary sat back and stared at S'rybe. "That must be hard for you. I don't think I would like always knowing what someone is thinking."

"Oh, it's not always fun. Most of the time I can shut out people when I want to but not you. You just about blow my head off when you aren't even thinking hard."

"Sorry," Mary said and pushed her plate away. There was just no use trying to eat. She was much too worried.

When everyone had finished eating S'ube stood and said to the guests, "If you are finished eating it would be my pleasure to have you join us in the entertainment area."

The entertainment room was directly across from the main entrance and was a little smaller than the room where they ate. Scattered around the room were tables and several benches and couches.

S'rybe took Mary by the hand and lead her to one of the tables. We can pretend to play 'Pebbles' while we talk.

Mary sat down, looked at the board and pebbles and said, "I know this game. Granny and I used to play it all the time but we called it 'Copo'."

"Good. We can play and talk then."

S'rybe and began to set up the board and held out the white pebbles to Mary. "I'll let you have the white pebbles."

Mary took the pebbles with a shaking hand.

S'rybe smiled and said, "Don't worry Mary. I told you I wouldn't tell your secrets."

"I know S'rybe but I can't help it. What would you do if you were me?"

"Oh, that's easy. I would just let my Mom know where I was and ask her to come and get me."

"But I can't," Mary said.

"Why not?" S'rybe asked, with a puzzled look."

"I just can't. I can't reach her."

"Mary, I don't believe you can't. Even blank people can communicate with their mothers."

"Blank people?"

"You, know, somebody with no talent. But you sure aren't blank. I don't understand why you think you can't talk to your mother."

"Granny said it was because I never bonded with my mother. She sent me away when I was a little baby."

"Know what I think? I think you could reach a tree if you set your mind to it, much less your own mother. Have you really, really tried?"

"No not really."

"Why?"

"Well," Mary said, "I'm afraid to try."

"Afraid! Afraid of your mother, how could you be afraid of your mother? Your mother is a wonderful person. Everyone on Ayri loves her. She is a wonderful ruler."

"I'm not afraid of her, I'm just afraid she won't believe I am her child. And," Mary paused to wipe a tear from her eye, "Maybe even if she does believe I am her daughter she might not want me."

"I can't believe your own Mother would not want you," S'rybe said pounding the table for emphasis.

"Sure that's easy for you to say, you have always been with your mother but my mother hasn't seen me since I was a little baby."

"So…you think she won't know you? Know what I think? I think she will know you. I bet she feels your presence even now and is worried about you."

Mary felt a lump in her throat and struggled not to cry. She had come a long way and been through so much and now that she was so close she was more scared than ever. S'rybe got up and went around to Mary and hugged her.

"Mary, don't cry. I just know it will be all right. I have a good feeling about it and my feelings are never wrong."

"I hope you are right," Mary managed to say.

Biz, who had been quietly watching flew over and snuggled on Mary's shoulder, cooing in her ear.

"Look!" S'rybe said, "Even Biz knows it will be alright. He is trying to tell you."

"You can tell what he is saying?" Mary asked in amazement.

"No, only you can do that. I just meant that he looks like he thinks it will be all right. Now, stop crying. We need to get away from everybody. Just follow my lead."

"All right," Mary said struggling to regain her composure."

S'rybe got up from the table, and stretched with a yawn. "Mom, I think Mary and I will go to bed now. We really are too tired to play."

S'rybe went to first her mother and then her father for a good night hug and waited at the doorway for Mary. Mary carefully shielded her thoughts and crossed the room to Granny and gave her a quick hug. She started to move away but Granny held her tight.

"Mary, I don't know what you and S'rybe are up to but please be careful."

"I will Granny."

S'rybe's room was located along the curved outer wall and had a small window high up the wall. There was a short curved table was placed against the wall with a sleeping mat next to it. An extra sleeping mat had been brought in for Mary. The girls sat cross-legged facing each other on S'rybe's mat.

"S'rybe, I don't know if I should try to do this. Granny thinks it is too dangerous for me to try to contact my Mother."

"I don't understand why it would be dangerous for you to ask your Mother for help. She needs you now. Everybody needs you. I don't know much about things but I have heard my parents talking. They said that the spirit of our people is low because of this long war with the Bahadin and the ruler does not a female child to follow her. Did you know there has always been an Heir Apparent? Our people are saying that this must be a sign that our planet is doomed. You don't know how much you mean to us!"

"Oh, S'rybe, I don't know. I'm just a kid. I'm not even sure I am the Heir Apparent."

"Well, I'm sure," S'rybe said, "I have never felt a power as strong as yours. You must be of the royal family because they always are the most powerful Thayers.

Now, listen to me. Close your eyes and think of your mother. Picture her in your mind. When you feel her presence you will be able to talk to her. No one else will be able to hear you, but it is possible that sensitive Thayers will feel your power. Don't worry about that right now."

Mary, grasped S'rybe's hand and smiled. "Alright. I will try."

Mary closed her eyes and concentrated. She pictured the beautiful red-haired lady that had comforted her in her dreams so long ago. At first she thought her attempt to reach her mother had failed, but slowly she began to feel the warm glow of her mother's love spread throughout her brain and the image of her mother became clear. For a moment she was lost in the sensation of comfort and peace and then she heard a voice so clearly as if her mother was sitting beside her. *L'demi, my beautiful child, how is it that I am finally hearing your thoughts?*

Mother, Mary thought, trying very hard to control her turbulent emotions, *I have been far away for a long time, but now I have come home.*

Home? You are here? But why have you traveled here, it is not safe.

The Bahadin found me where I was hiding on Earth. We barely escaped. I have been traveling for a long time.

Mary, where are you? How did you get to Ayri? I haven't had any report of a ship landing on the surface.

Mary felt her Mother's concern and more importantly her love. She tried to remain calm but it was hard.

It's a long story but we couldn't land in our ship because you would have ordered it blown out of the sky. We were in a warship my friends captured from the Bahadin. We landed a shuttle in the desert.

Bahadin Warship? Shuttle in the desert? Mary, where are the CAMCIA? Why have they not brought you to me?

X'akara is with me but she doesn't know I have contacted you. She thinks it would be unwise because a traitor has betrayed me once and she is afraid there may be more.

Mary, where are you?

"S'rybe, she wants to know where I am."

S'rybe smiled. "Tell her your are at the marhom of S'ube and S'ramo in the Carmytri district."

I am with S'rybe in the marhom of S'ube and S'ramo in the Carmytri district.

Stay there. I will come for you.

What if X'akara will not believe I have talked to you?

Tell X'akara Eir Rentis Reim posatis wemonea. It is the code phrase I implanted in her memory bank before she left. She will know you have reached your true Mother.

Mary let out the breath she had been holding and sat back. "I can't believe it. I communicated with my Mother!"

"What did she say?" S'rybe asked.

"She said she was coming to get me! I've got to go find X'akara. She gave me a message for her."

"X'akara, your CAMCIA? Isn't she still out working on your transport?"

"I guess so. Can you help me find her?"

"We can't go out there at night by ourselves. You'll just have to wait until morning."

"I can't wait. I need to talk to her now!" Mary said wringing her hands.

"Mary, it's too dangerous. There are things out there that could kill you. I won't let that happen to you. Your Mom can't get here before morning anyway. What's the hurry."

"I don't know. I just feel like I have to go now!"

"Did your Mom order you to go immediately, Mary?"

"No, I don't think so, but I…I don't know. It just feels like I have to go right now!"

"Listen, Mary, I know you feel like you need to do what you mother asked but wait. She wouldn't want you to put yourself in danger so close to home after all she went through to keep you safe."

Mary signed and leaned back. "I guess you are right. I don't think I want to go out there in the dark."

"Good," S'rybe said, "Now lets get some rest. I'm really tired. We will go out there first thing in the morning, I promise."

Mary tried to sleep but she was just too excited. *Will this night ever end?* she thought. She turned over and tried to be still and quiet. She could hear S'rybe's even breathing and knew her friend was asleep. Finally long after S'rybe fell asleep, Mary drifted off into an uneasy sleep.

It seemed like she had only been asleep for a few minutes when she felt S'rybe shake her.

"Wake up Mary. It's morning. We can go get X'akara now."

Mary was instantly awake. They dressed and hurried quietly to the door.

"Be very quiet now. We don't want anyone to catch us."

The slipped quietly out of the room and into the main room. They tiptoed across the room to the outside door. S'rybe paused by the door and grabbed two cloaks from the pegs on the wall.

"Here, Mary we will need these. It's probably cold outside this time of morning."

They carefully pulled the door open afraid with each creak of the hinges that someone would stop them. They slipped outside and ran toward the field where they left the RAT the day before.

As the got closer Mary could see X'akara still working on the RAT.

"X'akara," Mary shouted, "I need to talk to you."

X'akara turned and said, "Mary, what are you doing out here?"

"I have to tell you something."

"What could be so important that you would have to come out here alone. Is something wrong at the marhom?"

"No," Mary replied excitedly, "Nothing is wrong, but I have a message from my mother for you."

"Your mother? Have you tried to contact your mother? You know that is dangerous! How could you positively identify this person communicating with you as your mother?"

"I just know." Mary said. She couldn't explain how she was so certain it was her mother.

"That is unacceptable, Mary. We must get you away from here before something happens to you."

X'akara reached for Mary to push her in the RAT when Mary shouted, "X'akara my mother said to tell you 'Eir Rentis Reim posatis wemonea'. "

X'akara stopped and slowly put Mary down. "You have contacted your mother. No other living person could have known what to tell me. What does she wish me to do?"

"She wants us to stay here. She said she would come and get us."

"Very well. Let us go prepare for her arrival."

Mary, X'akara and S'rybe turned and began the trek across the fields to the marhom.

"X'akara, what does 'eir Rentis Reim posatis wemonea mean'?" Mary asked. "I studied languages on the long journey here and I don't remember anything that sounded like that."

"It means 'The Heir Apparent must be protected'. It is the language of the ancient scholars of Ayri. Very few people know of its existence. That's why she used that phrase for our secret password."

"Wow. My mother must be very smart," Mary said, beaming with pride.

"Yes, your mother is very intelligent."

When they got back to the marhom, S'rybe's family had just discovered the girls were not in their room.

"Where have you been?" S'rybe's father said sternly.

"Father, we went to get X'akara. We have important news."

"You know you are not supposed to leave the marhom without permission. You could have been hurt. Why did you disobey me?"

"Father," S'rybe said, "I am sorry I disobeyed you, but you have to listen. The Sovereign Ruler of Ayri is on her way here right now."

"What kind of nonsense are you babbling, child?" S'ramo said.

"It's not nonsense, father. Mary is the Heir Apparent and her mother is on her way here to get her."

"S'rybe, you know very well there is no Heir Apparent."

"Yes, there is father, I…"

"S'rybe, go to your room. I will not tolerate this behavior!" S'ramo shouted. "You have let your imagination run away with you for the last time."

S'rybe burst into tears but she stood her ground, "Father, you have got to believe me. I'm not making this up."

X'akara who had watched the exchange stepped between S'rybe and S'ramo and said to the child, "Take Mary and go to your sleeping quarters. I will handle this."

X'akara watched the children walk away, then turned to S'rybe's father and said "Master S'ramo, if I might have a word with you I think I may be able to explain.

In their room Mary and S'rybe found Biz still sleeping soundly. "Well, he sure didn't miss me did he?" Mary said, trying to get S'rybe's mind off her father's wrath.

Biz woke up and stretched. He grinned at Mary and flew over the S'rybe and gently rubbed away her tears.

"He knows you are sad," Mary said, "He is trying to make you feel better."

S'rybe took the small barda in her hand and rubbed his tiny head.

"He is making me feel better. I don't know how because I am in more trouble than I have ever been."

"He has a way of doing that. I think it is because he knows it will all work out."

"Do you really think so?" S'rybe asked, "Do you really think my father will forgive me?"

"Sure, he will!" Mary answered. "When my mother arrives he will have to believe us."

S'ramo didn't believe their story but eventually with help from Granny and Amden X'akara was able to convince him that Mary was the Heir Apparent and that the Ruler of Ayri was definitely on her way to the marhom.

S'ube was shocked to learn of the Sovereign's eminent arrival and said, "Oh no, the house is a mess. "What do you serve the ruler? I have got to get ready, I haven't a thing to wear!"

S'ube eventually calmed down enough to decide what food to prepare and cleaned and dusted every surface in sight. Mary and S'rybe were underfoot in the house and finally S'ube said "S'rybe please take Mary and go out side!"

"Oh, my goodness, S'ramo, I just sent the Heir apparent out to play, what will the Sovereign ruler think?"

"Mary wasn't insulted, she seemed happy to get out of the way," S'ramo said, "but perhaps we should send X'akara to watch them. I hate to think what the Ruler would do to us if something happened to Mary."

Chapter 28

"When do you think she will be here?" Mary had just asked X'akara for the hundredth time when they heard a rumble in the distance.

"What was that?" Mary asked.

"Sounds like a big ship coming this way. I bet that's your mother!" S'rybe said. "I better go tell Mother and Father."

As the ship grew closer Mary could see it was indeed very big and was surrounded by hundreds of smaller ships flying in formation around it.

"Wow," S'rybe said. "I have never seen so many ships at one time."

Even S'ramo was impressed. "Well, I guess you really are who you say you are, Mary."

"Yes, I guess I am", Mary said.

The gigantic ship hovered above the ground and then slowly descended, as huge supports extended from the bottom. The ship settled on the supports and the roar of the engines quieted. A ramp extended to the ground and a door at the top of the ramp silently slid open. A squad of armored CAMCIA placed themselves at intervals along the ramp and around the bottom. Then as X'akara pushed Mary forward to the edge of the ramp a woman appeared at the top.

Mary knew instantly it was her mother but her legs had turned to jelly and she couldn't move. The moment she had waited so long for had finally arrived and she didn't know what to do. Then her mother smiled and opened her arms. Mary ran up the ramp and into her mother's embrace. Suddenly she was engulfed in the warmth of her mother's love and her tears began to fall.

"There, there, L'demi, don't cry," her mother said, "You will have me crying as well."

Biz, who was being squashed in Mary's pocket, squawked.

"Oh Biz, I'm sorry," Mary cried.

"You have a barda?"

"Yes, mother. He is Biz. Biz, this is my mother."

Biz flew up and landed on Mary's mother's shoulder and nuzzled her face.

"He likes you!" Mary said.

"I like him too. I am glad you have a barda. Now my little Diza will have a friend to play with."

"You have a barda too?"

"Yes, I do. She has been with me for a long time. She is just inside. Would you like to meet her?"

"Oh, yes. That would be great!" Mary said as they went through the door, and entered the ship.

Mary's mother led her into a large chamber with stuffed chairs anchored to the floor. The room was not what Mary imagined a Royal Chamber should be.

"Why, this looks just like a comfortable living room." Mary said with surprise.

"I spend quite a bit of time in this cabin when I am traveling. I wanted it to be as comfortable as possible."

Biz let out a loud chirp and flew straight at the little barda sitting on a perch in the corner of the room. He circled the perch three times and then landed on the other end of the perch. Diza answered his chirp and moved toward him. He dipped his head and she dipped hers. Then they both began chirping excitedly.

"I think they like each other," Mary said.

"I think so too," Mary's mother said, "I believe they may become good friends.

Then Mary remembered her friends waiting outside. "Mother, I almost forgot. My friends are waiting outside. Would you like to meet them?"

"Of course," Mary's Mother said, turning to the CAMCIA by her side, "Please tell L'demi's friends we will join them shortly."

Everyone was waiting outside near the ramp when Mary and her mother came out of the ship. Everyone bowed low except S'rybe who stood staring at the Ruler of Ayri with open-mouthed awe.

"Bow down S'rybe," S'ube whispered to her daughter.

Just as S'rybe started to bow Mary's mother smiled and said, "Please don't bow. It is not required."

Mary took her mother's hand and walked toward her friends.

"Mother, this is Granny Mer, and Amden and X'akara."

"Granny Mer and Amden, my daughter has told me so much about you. I am deeply indebted to both of you. X'akara it has been a long time since I sent my child with you. You have served my daughter well."

Then Mary introduced her mother to her new friends, "This is S'ube, S'ramo and their daughter S'rybe."

"I am also indebted to you for sheltering my daughter and most of all to S'rybe for encouraging L'demi to contact me."

"Your highness, thank you for your kind words. We would be honored if you would join us for refreshments in our humble home," S'ube said nervously.

"That would be delightful," L'Alie, Sovereign Ruler of Ayri answered.

S'ube and S'ramo led the royal party to their home and soon were put at ease by L'Alie. She was so friendly and pleasant to be around that everyone forgot that they were in the presence of the ruler of Ayri.

"You have a beautiful home and I have enjoyed the refreshments but we must be on our way back to the royal residence. Thank you for the food and most of all for sheltering my daughter. You will be rewarded."

"No reward is necessary. We were happy to help her," S'ramo answered.

"S'rybe, L'demi tells me you were most helpful. When L'demi has settled in you are invited to come for a visit."

"Wow, that would be great!" S'rybe said.

With that said they walked back to the ship and prepared to leave. When the ship lifted off it moved smoothly across the planet. The beautiful scenery below fascinated Mary.

"I can't believe I am really home," she said to Granny.

Granny smiled and hugged Mary, "I'm glad you have made it home. It truly is a beautiful place. It reminds me of my Quain."

When the royal party arrived in the capital city hundreds of people were waiting outside the royal residence, feeling that something special was about to happen in spite of the ruler's attempt to shield her excitement.

The ship landed close to the royal residence and they slipped, unnoticed through a private entrance. Once inside Mary's mother said to a servant CAMCIA "Please take Granny Mer and Amden to the guest suites. I am sure they would like to freshen up. We will join them for dinner in the private dining room later."

Mary hugged Granny and Amden before they went to their quarters and then her mother said, "L'demi, you must be tired as well. Would you like to rest for a while?"

"I'm much too excited to rest," Mary said.

"Well then would you like to a tour of the royal residence?"

"Could I?"

"Of course. It is your home now," her mother said with a smile.

Mary was impressed with the royal residence and all the beautiful rooms. There was much to see but her mother saved the most impressive room for last.

"L'demi," Mary's mother said as they walked into an extremely large chamber, "this is the throne room."

"Wow!" Mary exclaimed, "This is fantastic!"

The room was richly decorated with ornate paintings on the walls. Rows of straight back chairs faced a large chair, the likes of which Mary had never seen. It was carved out of an enormous crystal. On the seat was a red silk cushion with a matching cushion on the back. Rays of crystal cut into the back of the chair reached high above them. The chair glowed with a faint golden light. Though made of a hard material it appeared warm and comfortable.

"Is that your throne, Mother?" Mary asked in awe.

"Yes, it is mine for now but it will be yours someday."

"Mine, I don't know. I don't feel very royal," Mary said as she walked to the throne for a closer look.

"I think you will be just fine, L'demi," Mary's mother said and then turning to the CAMCIA standing by the doorway she said. Tell the people of Ayri that I wonderful news and I will address them soon."

"L'demi, your father is on his way back here from inspecting a new defense system half the way around the world. He should be back soon but while you wait would you like to meet your brother?"

"Yes, I would like to meet my brother, but I just remembered. I have already met my twin brother."

"You met your twin, but how?" L'Alie said as a wave of sorrow swept over her, "It hurts me to tell you this, Mary, but your twin brother died during a missile attack."

"I know he died, but I met his spirit just before he left this universe. He said 'tell our parents that I love them and I am sad to leave them but I have fulfilled my destiny and I go on to a better place.'"

"You truly must have communicated with his spirit. That is exactly what he would have said," Mary's mother said, "He was a kind and thoughtful person. He died helping his teacher during the attack."

"I would have liked to know him better," Mary said, "but at least I got to talk to him a little."

L'Alie sat for a moment as she remembered L'amie.

The door opened and a tall young man entered the room. Mary knew immediately that he was her brother. He quickly crossed the room and grabbed Mary and twirled her around in a bear hug.

"L'demi, I have been feeling your presence for days. I thought I was losing my mind. I'm so glad to finally meet the source of my feelings. You are the one that tormented my little brother."

"What, I never tormented anyone in my life!" Mary said.

"Oh yes you did. Every time you bumped your head or had a temper tantrum he felt it. He said it was hard not to think of you, but of course we had been told never do that because Mom was so afraid you would be found by the Bahadin."

"Well they did find me, but that's another story."

Mary felt as comfortable with him as if she had known him all her life. They spent the rest of the afternoon getting to know one another. They exchanged stories of their life but L'reg thought Mary's life was much more exciting.

"Wow, L'demi, you have had some great adventures! I wish I could have been with you."

Mary was a little nervous about meeting her father, but that was just as easy as meeting her mother and brother.

Mary knew he was her father the moment he stepped in the room. He was tall and handsome with warm brown eyes and dark hair. She noticed immediately that he looked familiar.

"You look just like "X'orige!" Mary exclaimed.

"Do you mean the CAMCIA that your mother sent with you? Yes, I suppose I do. He was patterned after me. A lot of the royal CAMCIA were made to appear similar to the royal family."

Mary and her family were together at last and they were enjoying their reunion when a CAMCIA announced, "The seamstress is in the fitting rooms. May I tell her when you will be ready for the fitting?"

"Yes," L'Alie answered, "L'demi and I will join her in the fitting room in a few moments."

Mary went with her mother to the fitting room after receiving hugs and kisses from her brother and father.

"We'll see you later," they said as Mary left the room.

The seamstress placed Mary in front of a screen and adjusted it to Mary's height.

"What type of clothing will Your Highness need today?" the seamstress asked.

"She needs a full set of casual wear now. She will need a complete set of clothing including full ceremonial royal raiment within the next few days," L'Alie answered.

"Very well, Your Highness. I will have it ready in just a few moments. I took the liberty of selecting appropriate fabrics while I was waiting for you."

Mary was amazed to see a full set of clothing emerging from an opening in the machine only moments after her measurements were scanned.

"How did you do that?" she asked in awe.

"It is a computer guided sewing device. It makes a completed garment in minutes if the patterns are entered correctly."

The next few days went by quickly. While Mary was busy getting to know her family Granny and Amden made contact with the ship and were making arrangements to bring the huge warship down for the engineers and scientists to examine.

"Oh Biz!" she said, "I'm so happy! All my life I wanted a loving family and now I have one. It's almost too good to be true."

Mary was in her room surrounded by the dolls and toys that the royal family had given her. Looking around at the wonderful things she said, "I wish S'rybe could be here. She'd love all the beautiful dolls."

Mary's mother smiled at her beautiful daughter from the doorway and said, "S'rybe will be here tomorrow for the ceremony."

"What ceremony?" Mary asked.

"Don't worry about that now. I'll explain later," she answered.

Chapter 29

The next day Mary's mother found Mary staring out her window anxiously awaiting the arrival of S'rybe and her parents.

"When will S'rybe be here, Mother?"

"She will be arriving soon. You will have plenty of time to visit with her after the ceremony. You need to get ready, Mary. I've assigned a clothing matron to help you dress and I will come for you when I have finished dressing."

Mary wasn't used to being dressed by someone but she was glad for the help as she looked at the puzzling number of garments.

First to go on were the undergarments that were made of the softest material that Mary could imagine. Next Mary was helped to put on a long, gossamer iridescent dress that changed colors when she moved. Over that the matron placed a short cape trimmed in white iridescent material. Finally the matron brushed Mary's hair and placed a tiny tiara on her head.

When at last she stood in front of the mirror she was amazed at the transformation.

"Wow I look just like a princess!" she said to the clothing matron.

"Of, course Your Highness," the matron answered with a smile.

Mary was admiring her beautiful outfit in the mirror and laughing at the antics of Biz when she heard the door open and her mother came in the room dressed in an outfit that matched Mary's. Her barda flew quietly by her side. She swept across the floor and hugged Mary. Biz flew up and greeted the other barda with a cheerful chirp.

"I'm glad Diza and Biz have become friends. She can keep Biz company while we are busy with our ceremonies today."

Mary' mother went to her and held her at arm's length and said, "My sweet child, you are so beautiful. I have dreamed of this day for so long. I have lost too many years of your life and you have suffered many perils. I only hope you can forgive me. Perhaps I was wrong to send you away, but I was so afraid for you," she said her voice breaking.

"Please, Mother, don't cry. I understand. We will just have to make up for lost time now that we are together."

"Yes, yes, we will. I would love to stay here with you but duty calls. We must go tell our people that you are here," she said, "although, I think that they have already felt your presence. I felt a ripple of power flow across the world on the day you arrived and I'm sure that everyone did, even if they didn't know from whom it came."

"What do I have to do?" Mary asked nervously.

"I will present you to the people and perform the Ceremony of the Heir Apparent. Then you will address the people."

"You mean make a speech?" Mary managed to say, her throat threatening to close at the very thought.

"Yes, but you only have to say a few words. You will be fine."

"But, I don't know what to say."

"Don't worry, just say what is in your heart. It will come to you," she said as she led Mary to the door. "We must go to the balcony now."

L'Alie led Mary through the corridors and much too soon for Mary they stood at the entrance to the balcony. The balcony was actually a large open stage. Mary could see that Granny, Arman, Amden, S'rybe, S'ube and S'ramo were seated on one side of the balcony with X'orige and X'akara standing behind them. In the center of the balcony sat the large throne made of crystal. The chair glowed and sparkled in the sunlight as if lighted by some internal fire.

"Wow, is that your throne, Mother? It looks different out in the sunlight."

"It is my throne now, but in just a little while it will be yours as well. Stay here until I signal for you to join me on the balcony," Mary's mother said, bending down to give Mary a kiss. "Don't be afraid. When you get out there you will feel the love of the people of Ayri."

Mary swallowed and tried to be brave. *This is worse than being attacked by the slime people,* she thought.

L'Alie, Sovereign Ruler of Ayri stepped out on the balcony and a cheer rose from the crowd below. She walked to the center of the balcony and began speaking softly. There didn't appear to be any kind of microphone but her voice carried to everyone in the crowd.

"Today I come to you with the most wonderful news that it has ever been my pleasure to announce. I know that many of you have been troubled by the lack of an Heir Apparent and feared for the fate of our world. I am here today to inform you that the Heir Apparent and her twin brother were born to me many years ago during one of the first battles of our war against the Bahadin as they were storming the royal residence. I feared for her life and so to protect her I sent her far away. I was only able to withstand the pain of separation by reminding myself that she was safe. Now she has returned to claim her rightful place. So it is with great pleasure that I present to you my daughter, L'demi."

Mary's mother motioned to her and with shaky legs Mary walked out onto the balcony. There was complete silence as Mary's Mother led her to the throne and turned Mary to face the crowd.

"In the ancient test of the true Heir Apparent, my daughter will sit for the first time upon the throne of the Sovereign."

Mary sat down on the chair. She wasn't sure what to expect but almost immediately she felt warmth radiate throughout her body. Slowly the chair began to vibrate and glow with a golden light. Millions of tiny red, green, blue and gold sparks shot from the tips of the crystal rays as a thunder of jubilant music filled the air. The crown burst into cheers as waves of joy washed over Mary.

When the music had reached its peak and the fireworks slowed Mary leaned over close to her mother and said, "This is fantastic. Does this chair do this every time someone sits on it?"

"No, not for everyone," Mary's mother answered with a smile, "the chair will only respond to the Sovereign Ruler and her Heir Apparent."

The applause and joyous shouts from the audience went on for several minutes but slowly hushed when Mary's mother walked to the front of the balcony.

"Citizens of Ayri, I am honored to present to you the True Sovereign Heir Apparent, L'Demi!"

Once again the crowd broke into thunderous shouts of joy and applause.

Mary's mother turned to her and said, "Mary, please come forward and speak to your people."

"But I still don't know what to say."

"Just say what is in your heart."

Mary walked to the front of the stage. Suddenly the nervousness that she had felt was gone, replaced by a calm radiating from her mother and the joy being transmitted from the crowd.

"Contenza," she began, "I'm very happy to be home at last. The journey was a long and difficult one, filled with many dangers. I would never have made it back if it hadn't been for the CAMCIA that cared for me and the friends I found along the way. They are here with me today and I would like to introduce them to you. First the CAMCIA that cared for me and saved my life many times, X'akara, and X'orige."

X'akara and X'orige moved to a place just behind Mary amid the applause of the people.

Then Mary smiled at Arman and said, "This is Arman, he risked his life to come and rescue me after my ship was destroyed by space pirates."

The people cheered as Arman moved to stand with Mary.

Then Mary motioned to Amden and she said, "This is Amden who helped X'orige overthrow a Bahadin Warship and then helped bring me home."

The roar from the crowd was deafening as he moved to stand with Mary and Arman.

"When I finally got to this planet I was sheltered and fed by this wonderful family, S'ube, S'ramo and my dear friend, S'rybe."

They joined the group beside Mary. When the applause subsided Mary continued, "And last of all I would like to introduce Esmera of New Quain." Mary motioned for Granny to join her at the front of the balcony. "She gave me love and comfort when I thought no one could love me. She taught me many things and risked her life and her home to rescue me when I was shipwrecked."

Mary hugged Granny and again turned to face the people, her people she realized. She was about to continue when she heard a familiar chirp. Biz, who never could resist showing off flew on stage and circled Mary's head, settling down to scold Mary for not introducing him.

"Oh and this little fellow is Biz. He is my companion and friend who cheered me and comforted me and taught me how to have fun."

Mary turned to her friends and said, "Thank you. If not for you I would never have made it home!"

The people cheered for Mary's friends and for Mary. It was quite a while before they calmed enough for Mary to continue.

"A long time ago on a planet far away, I was known as Mary Smith. I thought my name and my life were plain and ordinary and it would always be that way. Since then I have been on many adventures and learned I had another name and that I was a princess and a Thayer, but in the end it seems to me that I am still Mary Smith. So, if it pleases the people and my family, I would still like to be called Mary."

Mary's mother paused for a moment and then placed her hand on Mary's shoulder and said, "So be it. From this day forth she shall be known as Mary, Sovereign Heir Apparent of Ayri.

The End

About the Author

Linda Tilley worked in the health care field as a radiology secretary until 2001 when she quit to write full time. Mary Princess of Ayri is her first novel and she wrote it because, in her words, "Little girls need heroes too". Linda lives in Lawsonville, North Carolina with her husband Joe and their three cats. She is currently working on her next novel.

Printed in the United States
1455400006B/102